Book One of Juxtan

Tricia Owens

Cover Art by Kellie Dennis at Book Cover by Design
www.bookcoverbydesign.co.uk

ISBN: 1508833419
ISBN-13: 978-1508833413

DEDICATION

Many people have made this book possible through their support and encouragement. The readers of Juxtapose Fantasy gave life to these characters and inspired me to keep going even on the darkest of writing days.
This book is for them.

The Sorcerer's Betrayal

CHAPTER ONE

"Caledon, catch!"

The blond-haired mercenary flicked out a dagger and deftly speared the thrown apple. He inclined his head at the green-eyed girl beside the fruit cart. "Many thanks, Mistress Alena." He smiled when she blushed, causing the freckles on her face stand out in sharp relief. He took a bite of the apple and approached her. Taking her hand, he pressed some coins into it. "Treat your man to a feast at one of the inns tonight, love. You two deserve a nice night out."

"Oh, Caledon, you don't need— "

He curled her fingers over the coin. "Sorry, love. Can't take them back once they've left my possession."

The red-haired girl colored again but nodded shyly. "Thank you, Caledon. You're a sweetie."

"Why are the ladies always telling you that?"

Caledon rolled his eyes at the familiar voice. Throwing a last wink at the girl, he turned to face the newcomer. A tall, lanky man with dirty blond hair and mellow brown eyes was currently grinning at him from the middle of the street. Mercenary that he was, he was dressed like Caledon in shades of black. However, instead of carrying the various daggers that Caledon did, the lanky man wore only a single sword sheathed over his shoulder.

"They always say that because it's true," Caledon replied after emitting a long-suffering sigh. "Maybe if you possessed half as much charm you'd fare the same way, Tye."

The other man laughed, his tobacco-stained teeth spread wide. "Charm and a lack of discrimination. You best me in both."

Caledon shrugged. His preferences in bed were no secret. "I appreciate a pretty face. Gender is beside the point."

"Hmm. So I suppose you'd be interested in that walking beauty."

Caledon followed his friend's knowing gaze to a tavern several yards away. Stepping from its doors was a raven-haired creature of such unexpected beauty that Caledon forgot to blink.

"By the gods," he breathed, his gaze riveted to the slender figure that were it not for the gait, he might have mistaken for a female. Shoulder-length black hair framed a face whose alabaster skin suggested a life spent indoors. The stranger's high, graceful cheekbones were almost exotic in this place where classic beauty was near unheard of. And his eyes... Caledon felt his body stir. Even from the distance he could see that the stranger had impossibly wide grey eyes the color of storm clouds and rain. "Amazing. Who is that?"

Tye laughed, stepping beside him to join in his study of the stranger. "He's in Rhiad recruiting men for a temporary army his father is trying to build. Seems there's a dispute that needs a few sharp swords to settle. The usual." He elbowed his friend meaningfully. "I spoke with him earlier this morning. He's even more breathtaking up close. You should meet him."

"It was never a question," Caledon replied distractedly as he watched the stranger cross the street and enter Caledon's favorite tavern. "What is his name?"

"Hadrian."

The Bell and Buckle was Caledon's favorite place to relax in Rhiad because it was the closest thing to sitting in the sun. The tavern possessed more windows than any other building in town: four, to be exact—two on either side of the front door and one in each of the side walls. When he sat at the bar stretched across the back he could almost imagine himself outdoors. Or at least, that's what Caledon liked to tell himself. Since he invariably spent the majority of his waking hours either working in the pitch black of night or lurking about in the shadows of the seediest places imaginable, when his time was his own he sought the light. He wanted to cleanse himself, if only for a little while, of the darkness.

Today the B&B was his favorite tavern for another reason. It was where his quarry had gone. Having followed the dark-haired stranger inside, Caledon now lounged at the bar, surreptitiously watching him from over the rim of a mug full of foamy ale.

Gods, but when had anyone walked into Rhiad looking as this one did? Caledon traveled extensively as his jobs warranted, but always it seemed he ended up lurking in places where dirt was the cosmetic of choice and baths were few and far between. Caledon had grown accustomed to dirty faces and questionable hygiene. Seeing someone like this stranger, whose clean garments and well-groomed appearance indicated that he obviously came from a far different background, was worth staring at even if he wasn't handsome.

But to Caledon's immense enjoyment the stranger was nothing less than stunning. His long dark hair was the shade of a raven's wing, thick and glossy. Contrasted against his charcoal tunic and grey cloak the stranger's fair skin look almost translucent. Caledon's eyes traveled up the stubborn jaw and full, pink-petaled lips, tracing the high arc of cheekbones until they came to the stranger's gaze. He needed to see those magnetic eyes up close.

"You takin' a bite of what he's offerin', Caledon?"

The mercenary nearly choked on his ale, quickly wiping at his chin. He turned on the stool and regarded the barkeep with a cocked brow. "I assume that was deliberate, Rankin. Are you trying to make me waste good ale by spilling it all over myself?"

Rankin, who owned the Bell and Buckle, shrugged innocently. "Just means you gotta buy more." He picked up a dirty rag, moved it around in his hands until he found a patch that wasn't as dark as the rest, and used it to wipe out a mug. He inclined his head towards the stranger in the corner. "You goin' to talk to him? Heard he's lookin' to hire."

"Mmm," Caledon murmured noncommittally, spinning around to regard the man in question again. "Who's he talked to so far?"

"Everyone. Doesn't seem to care 'bout skill or price. Seems like he just wants bodies. He'd probably want yours."

Caledon rolled his eyes at the innuendo. "Never were one for subtleties, were you, Rank?"

The barkeep snorted. "Like you weren't thinkin' the same thing when you followed him in here."

Caledon laughed. All right, so he had a reputation. It wasn't something he was about to change. He enjoyed his life for the most part. Caledon lived to live. That meant enjoying the more pleasant aspects of life as often as possible.

It was an attitude he had long ago learned to adopt. Killing people for a living wasn't the most heartening of occupations. He found himself in unsavory positions more often than not. And sometimes it took more ale and sex than was probably healthy to make himself forget what he had willingly committed for a bag of coin. He had a conscience somewhere deep down. But if he tried hard enough, he could almost make himself forget it.

Someone like this stranger was the perfect means of doing so.

"Gonna make yourself available to 'im?" Rankin asked with a smirk as Caledon slid off the stool.

Caledon threw a grin over his shoulder. "In every way possible, my friend."

Hadrian decided that he didn't much care for this place. Not just this tavern which reeked of sweat and and old ale, but the entire town of Rhiad. This was why he never left the island of Shard's Point. Why should he, when this was all there was to look forward to?

He took a tentative sip of his ale and suppressed a grimace. Was his father punishing him for something? Is that why Hadrian had been chosen for this task when any member of the Order could have accomplished the same? Hadrian wouldn't be surprised if that was the case. Since he could remember, his life had consisted of him attempting not to displease his father and inevitably failing. Somewhere, somehow, he had done something wrong yet again. Now he was trapped here with what must surely be the scum of the land collected for his perusal.

Hadrian rubbed at his forehead idly, thinking on the men he had encountered during this mission. Killers, all of them. Why his father needed to employ them he had no idea, nor would he ask. He had learned long ago that simply being the great Gavedon ni Leyanon's son did not mean he was privy to the man's mind. Hadrian was as much a stranger to his father's inclinations as the rest of the members of the Order. Every day he was reminded of that fact as Gavedon's eyes looked through Hadrian as though he didn't exist.

He looked up as the chair directly across from him was

slid away from the table. A man's booted foot had pulled it back and now rested upon its seat. Hadrian's eyes traveled up the muscled leg clothed in worn, black breeches. Daggers were strapped on either side of the man's thigh and another one hung at his waist. The strap of a sheath ran across the front of the man's dark tunic, drawing the fabric tight over a broad chest. Hadrian could see the smooth hilt of a sword peeking over the man's shoulder. A mercenary. A well-armed one, at that.

Then his eyes lifted to the man's face and Hadrian at once forgot his dislike of Rhiad.

"I've heard you're looking to hire a few swords," the man said in a lazy drawl, his voice deep and nuanced.

Something wild fluttered in Hadrian's stomach. He didn't understand the sudden tightness in his chest that made it difficult to draw breath. The man before him was not much older than he but the tiny lines around his bright blue eyes spoke of an experience far beyond Hadrian. He was well traveled; Hadrian surmised as much from the deeply tanned skin and the straw-colored hair that held pale strands of sunlight. He had a strong, square face that Hadrian sensed could look frighteningly dangerous should the moment warrant it. But right now the man was grinning at him with wide white teeth that looked even brighter set within his dark countenance.

Hadrian realized he was staring. He felt heat steal into his cheeks and that only made the man's smile widen further. Someone who definitely knows how handsome he is, Hadrian decided, dropping his eyes. And most likely with the charm to match. Hadrian might not have had much experience dealing with the outside world but he had come to recognize those few to whom charm came second nature. Conscious of his own lack of social skills, he had learned to be wary of them.

"Are you a mercenary?" Hadrian asked him as calmly as he could. He wanted to wipe his sweating palms against his breeches but feared it would reveal too much to the man.

Those blazing blue eyes looked unerringly sharp.

"For a price," the man replied.

"The very definition of a mercenary, is it not?" Hadrian said, glancing up at him. The man was still smiling and watching Hadrian with undisguised curiosity. Cursing his fair skin that betrayed too much, Hadrian shrugged. "Money is not an issue."

"Money is always an issue." The booted foot lifted from the chair. "May I sit?"

The prospect of having the man join him was both daunting and exciting. Hadrian nodded, trying to appear unaffected. He knew he failed by the amusement that creased the mercenary's face as he lowered himself into the chair and leaned both forearms on the table between them. The man had rolled up the sleeves of his tunic allowing Hadrian to see the muscles of his forearms flex beneath the light dusting of golden hair. Hadrian quickly looked away.

"Why are you trying to appear disinterested in me?" the man asked.

"What—what do you mean?" Hadrian stammered, caught aback.

A twitch of the lips showed the other man had caught his slip. "You need men for your father's army, don't you?" the mercenary said, cocking his head innocently. "And you've said that money is not a problem for you."

Frowning with the fear he was being played with, Hadrian sat back to build some distance. "If you're willing then yes, I wish to hire you. My father needs every mercenary in Rhiad."

The other man steepled his fingers, his sky-blue eyes looking over them at Hadrian. "What is it you're hiring for, exactly?"

Would that I knew, Hadrian thought somewhat resentfully. Aloud, he said, "My father owns a great deal of land in northern Jeynesa. It's been in his family since beyond memory, passed to the eldest son of each generation. However, an illegitimate son has surfaced to contest my father's claim." Hadrian leaned forward again, trying to appear concerned. "My father has been facing threats of violence and he fears serious fighting. He sent me here to gather enough mercenaries to form a small army. I think he hopes that a show of force will forestall any actual confrontation. Therefore, I need men like you."

The words, given to him to repeat by Gavedon, and having been used countless times already, suddenly sounded transparently false as he spoke them to this mercenary. Maybe it was because the blue eyes that watched him as he spoke didn't blink. He sensed that this man wasn't a fool. It made him add, "My father will be here in a fortnight to explain everything. You may decide then whether or not you wish to remain in his employ. I don't particularly care if you don't trust me."

Hadrian knew he was taking a risk. He wasn't supposed to leave the option to refuse. Gavedon had impressed upon Hadrian the importance—no, the urgency—of ensuring that every mercenary in the town be convinced to meet with Gavedon. But Hadrian was unnerved by this mercenary's confidence. He was different than the others Hadrian had already spoken to who had radiated various degrees of danger and recklessness. This man's threat seemed layered in something else that Hadrian didn't quite recognize.

"You're a bit swift to jump to conclusions," the mercenary said with a laugh. It was an easy laugh that Hadrian sensed came often. Some of his tenseness fled at the light sound. "I never said I don't trust you. I simply don't know you. Yet," he added with a grin. "My name is Caledon ni Agthon."

Hadrian found it disconcerting that the man could look so open and friendly when he was obviously a paid killer. Still, Hadrian did manage to relax somewhat. "I'm Hadrian."

He hoped he didn't sound overly suspicious by not

giving his surname but Caledon did not seem to mind. The mercenary smiled with genuine warmth. "Now forgive me if it is I who is jumping to conclusions, Hadrian, but I'd wager you don't venture into the likes of Rhiad very often, do you?"

Hadrian nodded, intending to play up his role as the spoiled, sheltered son of a wealthy land owner. "I am unused to such... places, yes. But this is important to my father, so I will deal with it as I must."

Caledon's eyes glittered. "Your father must have great faith to send such a lamb to the wolves."

Except this lamb is no mere lamb, Hadrian thought. Revealing his true nature though, was out of the question. Gavedon had made that painfully, memorably clear. "I suppose my father thinks the prospect of future wealth under his employ will dissuade anyone from murdering me outright. Better to hold out for a future reward that is sweeter."

Caledon grinned. "Oh, yes," he murmured, eyes intent on Hadrian. "Anticipation is much sweeter."

Flustered by the interest he saw in the blue eyes, Hadrian could not hold Caledon's gaze. Reactions like those of the other man's were something Hadrian had been trying hard to understand since stepping onto the mainland. Perhaps it was his admittedly odd coloring or maybe it was his garments that clearly marked him as a stranger, but he had been subject to more attention in the last five days than he could remember receiving in his entire life.

"Don't look so uneasy," Caledon said gently. "If I intend to work for you I'm not going to attack you. You needn't be afraid of me."

Hadrian wanted to laugh. He wasn't afraid of being attacked by the blond-haired mercenary. Not when he knew that with a softly spoken word he could send the larger man flying through the air and across the room. What made him uncomfortable was that deep down he understood that Caledon presented a threat to him that he had had little experience countering.

Hadrian had never before considered his secluded upbringing to be a burden. What did it matter if his contact with those outside the Order was limited to a handful of fanatics? But now, forced to interact with the mainland, he glimpsed one of the ways in which such social inexperience would leave him vulnerable.

"Doesn't your father worry that you might be kidnapped and held for ransom?" Caledon asked. "You're making it far too obvious that you come from a family of wealth. To those less scrupulous than I you're something of a temptation." He smiled. "In many ways."

Hadrian shifted in his chair uneasily, wishing the other man were ugly or rude or anything other than what he was so that Hadrian would want to conclude their business. But Caledon was handsome and charming and seemed genuinely interested in him...Would it hurt to indulge in the man's attention? Gavedon's face rose in his mind. Yes, it would.

"I can take care of myself; you needn't concern yourself on that matter," Hadrian replied.

Before he could react, Caledon's hand shot across the table and grabbed hold of his wrist, turning his palm up on the table. Hadrian tugged halfheartedly as a calloused fingertip drew lightly across the skin of his palm. His eyes widened at the bolt of sensation that the small touch sent through his body. He held his breath as Caledon drew a lazy circle in his palm.

"You aren't proficient with the sword," the mercenary commented as he watched his finger trace the contours of Hadrian's palm. "You ride often enough but your hands are too soft for you to convince me you're adept with weapons, love." He raised blue eyes to study Hadrian. A small smile played at the edges of his lips. "So tell me how it is that you take care of yourself, hmm? Because I wouldn't want to see a pretty thing like you get hurt. Not if

I could have prevented it."

Love. Pretty thing. Hadrian stared at Caledon, stunned at the casual endearment, the lazy compliment.

He frowned slightly when Caledon released his wrist.

"You need someone to watch your back while you're in Rhiad."

Hadrian mentally shook his head, clearing his senses as the words sank in. "What are you talking about?"

Caledon shrugged, sitting back in his chair. The pale light picked out the highlights in his hair, making Hadrian want for the first time in his life to touch someone else. "That coy little game of yours might work for you in your social circles when your father is around, but it's guaranteed to make you a target in a place like this. For some men, nothing is quite as seductive as the chance to 'break' someone like you."

Hadrian felt the heat rising in his cheeks. He didn't want to be having his conversation. Though he didn't fully understand all of Caledon's references he could guess at their meanings.

"I'm not playing at anything," he insisted, dragging his hand into his lap and scrubbing at his palm to erase the mercenary's touch. "And I don't need your assistance. I will only be here another three days. I shall be fine."

Caledon merely smiled.

Becoming irritated, Hadrian squared his jaw. "You're not the only one I need to speak to while I'm here. My time is short. I have others I see. May I count you among those interested in my father's employ? As I said, he will be here in a fortnight to explain everything further."

Caledon sat back, studying him thoughtfully. "Why the haste? The sun hasn't set yet. We've time to share conversation. You're like a skittish maiden."

Hadrian knew the comment was deliberately intended to provoke him. He forced himself to ignore it, unwilling—gods, afraid—to engage this dangerous man further. Hadrian was out of his element and they both knew it.

"I haven't come to Rhiad to share in conversation," he said carefully, making sure the mercenary understood every word. Only the memory of his father's mood kept him from looking away from Caledon's heated blue eyes. If Hadrian failed in this the punishment when he returned to Shard's Point would be unbearable."I'm sorry... Caledon, but I need to conduct my business." He hesitated, then recklessly added, "Maybe—perhaps we could meet another time."

He immediately blushed at his own forwardness. What was he doing? He would never come back here. And if his father found out he was—interested—in someone on the mainland, Hadrian would be forbidden from stepping foot off the isle again. But when Caledon's eyes lit up, a lazy grin curling his lips that shortened Hadrian's breath, Hadrian knew why he had said what he had. Because he hoped it would come true.

"Not today then," Caledon said, deliberately misunderstanding. Before Hadrian could clarify, the mercenary rose from his chair and came around the table. He braced a strong, tanned hand on the table beside Hadrian and leaned over him. Hadrian dropped his eyes to the table, afraid to look up into the blue gaze right beside his face. Caledon's breath was soft and warm against his cheek, stirring his hair. The rumble of his quiet voice against his ear made Hadrian's body flood with heat.

"I'm glad I met you, Hadrian. It's been a long time since I've encountered anyone like you." Rough fingertips brushed a strand of dark hair from Hadrian's temple. His lashes fluttered in unconscious response. "I'll see you again before you leave. I promise."

Something long repressed made Hadrian turn his head and blurt, "Will you?"

Momentary surprise was replaced by a lush confidence that had Hadrian's insides melting. Caledon's eyes lowered to Hadrian's mouth a moment before the mercenary's thumb brushed over it, slightly parting his lips. "I always keep my promises, love. And this is one I want to keep very badly." He stroked Hadrian's bottom lip. "Very badly, indeed."

Hadrian's heart was pumping so hard he feared it would explode. Oh, gods, he wanted to lick Caledon's thumb. He wanted to grab him and, and—what? Sadly, he didn't know what he wanted, just more of this luscious, blood-stirring feeling that was making him ache in all those secret places and left him hungry. Hungry for touch, for taste, for feelings...

He knew he was trembling by the way Caledon's eyes darkened as they looked over him. "Gods be damned," the mercenary said abruptly. "Meet me in the stables beside the Fickle Harper Inn."

Hadrian started to nod automatically, then stopped himself as reason began to intrude. "No, I—I can't. I need to meet too many—"

"Later tonight," Caledon breathed. "After you've had your supper. I want to see you."

Gods, if his father ever found out... But, found out what? What if the mercenary only wanted to speak with him? Ah, but what if he wanted more? Hadrian had little idea what that "more" could entail, but he wanted to find out.

He nodded, regretting the action as it dislodged the touch from his mouth. Caledon smiled faintly at his expression. "Meet me tonight and I'll give you more," the blond promised.

More. Whatever it was, Hadrian wanted it. His eyes locked on Caledon as the blond backed away and strode casually from the room. When the man had left, Hadrian ran a hand down his face. He was flushed with heat and his heart was still pounding. He almost smiled. He normally only felt this way when he magicked. He wondered if what he had just experienced with Caledon wasn't its own form of magick. He vowed to find out.

CHAPTER TWO

Rankin needed to clean his damn windows, Caledon thought sourly as he tried to see through the dirt and smoke-filmed glass. How in the hell was Caledon supposed to keep an eye on his newfound interest if he couldn't see him? Leaning against the side of the neighboring mercantile, he stretched his neck to better glimpse the latest interloper on Hadrian's table. Caledon scowled. All he could make out of the man was his grin, which was entirely too suggestive for Caledon's tastes. The man would have to go.

Before he could straighten away from the wall a hand caught his sleeve.

"Don't go causing trouble you don't need," Tye warned jovially. "You just met him. He might not be worth it."

Caledon shook his head. "He's worth it. I'd stab you in the back for a chance with him."

Tye pretended shock. "Me? I always suspected our friendship was thin but not that thin. Throw me over for a pretty face, eh? I'll remember that the next time you're arse-deep."

"I don't get it, Tye," Caledon mumbled, watching the new mercenary throw yet another leering grin at Hadrian. His hands fisted. "Something about him is getting to me. Like a burr in my shoe that keeps digging deeper with every step. It's like I don't want anyone else in Rhiad to even look his way. He's mine."

Tye whistled, settling against the wall beside Caledon. "Your words frighten me, my friend. You sound as though you're—dare I suggest it—falling in love?" He clutched at his chest melodramatically. "Surely the great Caledon hasn't succumbed at last to that fabled weakness."

Caledon leveled a glare at him hot enough to melt glass. "Don't make me run you through with my sword. Because believe me, continue on with this subject and I'll do it."

Tye smiled sympathetically. "Aw, come on, Caledon. Nothing wrong with falling in love. Even if it's with, well, a him." His eyes swung to the window Caledon was trying to stare through. "Granted, a very pretty him, but a him, nonetheless— "

"Your point?" Caledon said blandly.

The other mercenary shrugged, his expression sobering. "It's just I've never known you to really care about someone that way. You entertain several lovers, sure. And I hear you treat them well. But this...Well, it'd be nice to see you have a deeper interest, that's all."

Several lovers. That was an understatement. Caledon enjoyed his romps between the sheets. He knew he was a good lover and he enjoyed sharing his talents. Did that make him shallow? Did he care? So what if he never settled down with one person? He had his brothers to carry on the family line. All that was left for him of family duty was to not embarrass them all.

And Hadrian wasn't an embarrassment. Oh, no. He was a prize.

"I'm going to see him tonight," he told Tye, breathing a little easier when he saw the mercenary who had been speaking with Hadrian stand up from the table. "This may sound odd, but I get the impression that he doesn't engage in trysts very often."

"No wonder you're hooked," Tye teased. "Always were a sucker for a virgin."

The words sounded vaguely lecherous to Caledon and

that bothered him. "It's not just that," he protested. "It's something about him. He's different, he's— " Why by the gods was he trying to explain himself like some besotted maiden? "Ah, forget it." He pulled out his classic grin. "Once I poke him a few times I'll probably grow bored with him. It wouldn't be the first time I lost interest after a tumble."

No, not the first time, but he secretly doubted that it would be the case with Hadrian.

If Tye had similar doubts, he kept them to himself. "Yeah, maybe that'll happen. We'll see, huh?" He lightly punched the other man in the shoulder. "Just don't go starting fights over him just yet. That'd be a humiliating way to die, my friend."

"Don't worry," Caledon assured him. His eyes were so intent on Hadrian's latest guest that he didn't even see his friend leave. "I have no intention of dying before I get a taste of him."

By the time Hadrian exited the doors of the Mercenary Guild Caledon was ready to strangle someone simply to relieve the pressure. If he'd known the other man was going to the Guild he would have swiftly talked Hadrian out of it. The Mercenary Guild of Rhiad was nothing more than a house of whores. Run by a handful of former soldiers, the Guild hired out men like they were selling prostitutes. When they couldn't find enough mercenaries willing to take the meager cut being offered them, the Guild had no qualms about dragging in drunken wretches to play the part of "skilled swordsmen". As low down the social ladder as knew he was, Caledon still felt able to sneer down at the Guild.

Yet as he trailed Hadrian from a careful distance, Caledon began to reconsider. Hadrian might not even care about such details. Indeed, he hadn't asked a single question about Caledon's skills when he'd inquired about hiring him, which the mercenary found a bit odd. Still, it was an insult to think Caledon might be working alongside common Guild members. He'd have to have a word with Hadrian about that. Even he had his standards.

Unconsciously stepping from shadow to shadow in the deepening twilight, Caledon followed Hadrian to the docks. Hadrian had kept to the main byways of Rhiad during the day but now he was straying into more questionable territory. A rough crowd typically loitered at the docks and Caledon could just imagine the sort of reception someone with Hadrian's looks would receive. He kept his hand near the closest dagger.

True enough, as Hadrian paused at the end of a pier looking out over the purple water, a man approached him. He was a deckhand by the looks of it, taking a break from maintenance on a small schooner docked alongside the pier. Caledon stepped closer, watching carefully. He didn't want Hadrian to know he was being followed but he wasn't about to see that pretty face marred either.

The man said something and reached out to tug on Hadrian's hair. Hadrian turned slowly, looking strangely unconcerned at finding himself cornered by a much larger, stronger man. Caledon kept his weight on the balls of his feet, ready to spring forward at the slightest hint of fear from Hadrian. The deckhand spoke again and continued to fondle the younger man's dark hair.

Hadrian frowned and knocked the hand away. The deckhand growled something, his hand reaching up again. Caledon tensed. But Hadrian remained eerily calm. He said something very quietly and looked straight into the other man's eyes.

The deckhand started as if confronted by something unexpected and hastily dropped his hand. Caledon's brows creased. Hadrian didn't move, simply stared at the other man, yet whatever was in his eyes was powerful. The deckhand murmured something then quickly backed away.

He turned and stumbled down the pier until he came to the gangplank of his schooner. Caledon watched in confusion as the man scurried into the ship as though an angry mob were on his heels.

Now what, by the gods, had that been?

So thrown aback by what he'd witnessed, he neglected to conceal himself as Hadrian's gaze fell his way. The younger man's look of surprise and pleasure was quickly followed by wariness.

"Are you following me?" he demanded.

Caledon grinned to cover up his uneasiness. "Said I'd watch your back, didn't I?"

"I don't need you to," Hadrian replied impatiently.

"So I see." Caledon nodded towards the schooner. "What was that all about? He acted as though you're the carrier of some particularly foul plague."

Hadrian smiled faintly. "Maybe I am."

The small smile and the attempt at humor surprised Caledon. Hadrian had been too high strung to react this way to him earlier. Perhaps the younger man was becoming more comfortable in his presence. The thought was heartening.

Caledon took a step forward. "I hope you're not contagious," he said easily. Even with the setting sun at his back the slight widening of Hadrian's eyes was obvious as Caledon closed the gap between them. Caledon reached up and took a strand of dark hair between his fingers, for some reason wanting to mimic the deckhand's movements. Wanting to see if Hadrian's reaction would be the same, perhaps. "Because if you are contageious and it's transmitted through touch," Caledon murmured, gazing down at the younger man, "we may have a problem."

The grey eyes watched Caledon warily. "Why is that?"

Caledon stroked the silky lock of hair. "Because I want to touch every inch of you."

"You—" Hadrian dropped his eyes, a fierce blush spreading over his cheeks. The length of hair between

Caledon's fingers trembled. When had Caledon last made someone tremble without a touch? The reaction made him feel like the land's most potent lover. They hadn't done anything together yet. What would happen when they did? Caledon's skin broke out in tingles. He vowed to find out even if it killed him.

Hadrian took a step back, his hair slipping from between the mercenary's loose grasp. "Caledon," he began, his tongue struggling around the unfamiliar name, "I don't need you following me. I'm well able to take care of myself."

"Yes, you never answered how you do that." Caledon studied him. "What are you, a mage in disguise? Or worse, a sorcerer?"

Hadrian laughed thinly. "Would that be so bad?"

Caledon thought of his thief friends, Gam and Lio, who had been cursed by a sorcerer. "It would be a considerable disappointment," he replied drolly.

Something passed quickly over Hadrian's face. He looked away before Caledon could positively identify it. Caledon caught a handful of hair again, wanting badly to use the grip to bring the other man closer. But he only cupped the dark strands, letting them pool in his palm like black ink. "You're too fair to be a sorcerer," Caledon declared, rubbing his fingers together over the inkiness. "All the sorcerers I've ever encountered must have inadvertently misused their magick because gods, were they ugly. Hideous, really." He shuddered melodramatically.

Hadrian stared at him a moment, then broke into laughter. "That is the most ignorant thing I have ever heard anyone say," he said around his laughter. "Not all sorcerers are ugly."

"Really?" Caledon said, debating. "Unless you've one to show me who can change my mind I'm sticking by my opinion. Ogres, all of them."

Smiling, Hadrian shook his head, his hair slipping free

of Caledon's light grasp. The mercenary sighed at the loss. Hearing it, Hadrian gave a mystified smile. "I wish I understood the fascination with my hair. So many people seem to want a handful of it."

Caledon cocked a head as if considering. "Because it's clean."

Hadrian's face registered confusion. "What?"

"Well, you don't have lice that I can see. And so far no fleas... Quite an oddity in Rhiad, in case you hadn't noticed." His smile matched Hadrian's. "I consider myself an exception to the lot, of course."

Hadrian's light laugher followed Caledon as he moved past the younger man to the end of the pier. As though it were something he did every day, Caledon sat down upon the wood, letting his legs dangle over the side.

He could feel Hadrian hesitate beside him, uncertain whether to join him or continue looking down. "So that's your explanation?" the younger man asked. "You've a fascination with cleanliness?"

Caledon tilted his head back, resting its weight on his shoulders as he looked up. "You've hair the color of shadow, Hadrian. I'm rather intimate with the darkness myself. I'm drawn to it." And to you. Their eyes held for a heartbeat and Caledon thought he saw a darkening of the grey depths. "Come down here," he said, facing the water again, "you're hurting my neck."

Caledon gazed out at the rippling waters of Blackfell Bay, at the ribbons of purple and mauve that twisted over the surface. He realized he was holding his breath in anticipation of what Hadrian might do. He relaxed as Hadrian carefully lowered himself beside him a good arm's length away.

"I've heard that my mother had hair so pale it was nearly white," Hadrian said tentatively.

"That explains your complexion," the mercenary replied, letting his eyes drift over the other man's pale skin.

A stubborn frown creased the younger man's lips. "It

makes me odd," Hadrian argued, kicking his feet over the water. "People stare at me."

Caledon shook his head, amazed at the other's naiveté. Hadrian sounded more than sheltered, he sounded cloistered. Though he was the son of a wealthy land owner and surely the target of many a female hoping to make a good marriage, Caledon would wager his next meal that Hadrian had never even been kissed. Now there was a travesty worth amending. "People stare at you, yes. But not for the reasons you think, love."

Hadrian ducked his head in embarrassment. Caledon was entranced.

"May I—may I ask you something?" Hadrian said hesitantly.

Caledon tried to catch his eye but the grey gaze was skittish. He turned to study the sunset instead. "Of course."

Without the pressure of Caledon's gaze, Hadrian was able to look at the mercenary's profile. "Why are you here? Why... with me?"

Because you are the most fey creature I have ever met in my life, Caledon thought to himself. You have a beauty to weaken my knees and yet you are unaware of it yourself.

But such words might have scared the other man away so he said instead, "I find you refreshing. The work that I do can be ugly and dark. It's enough to make a man lose interest in that which used to make him happy. You, on the other hand, are the opposite of all of that. At the risk of sounding like I'm courting you —" *which I am,* " —you are the light that someone like me, yearns for."

He felt Hadrian's eyes roam his face like shy fingers. "If being a mercenary bothers you so much, why do you do it? You seem intelligent and your skills with weaponry must be considerable. Why not something else?"

Caledon shrugged, about to say something simple and only half-true to end this particular topic, then hesitated. "Do you really want to know?" He turned to look at the other man.

Hadrian nodded. "I do."

But Caledon shouldn't have met the other's eyes, because now he was able to see the earnestness in those wide grey pools. Those eyes wanted to know Caledon's secrets. They encouraged him to shed his concealing cloak of humor and admit that being a mercenary had not been his choice in life. That it had been something done out of a painful sense of righteousness. It was a righteousness that burned within him yet, but it grew dimmer with each morally questionable job he accepted. I do it for the coin, had always been his stock response, thrown out with a disarming grin. But Hadrian's eyes didn't accept that. They wanted him to tell that truth. And the truth was that Caledon had taken up the sword long ago to conquer an injustice. Now he wielded it only because he did not know what else to do. Though he would never admit it aloud, in his heart he feared he was no better than those who fought for the Guild.

But to admit that to Hadrian was pointless. There were other ways to woo a potential lover than to resort to the cold, hard truth no matter how well it might be received.

He reached out and wrapped dark hair around his fingers. The touch made Hadrian draw back some, like a tide that had reached too far up the beach. The demands of his eyes retreated as well.

"I haven't the imagination for anything better," Caledon told him lightly. "What I do keeps me in ale and whores and that's as much as I could ask for."

Disappointment shadowed Hadrian's eyes. "That's not what you were going to say," he said softly.

Caledon stared at him, feeling unexpectedly vulnerable. He didn't like it. The corner of his mouth twitched into a familiar smirk. "Ale and whores, love, really are all I care about. I'm very easy to please." He let his eyes roam the younger man's body. "You'll find that out soon enough, I think."

Hadrian frowned slightly. "I-I need to take my supper," he told Caledon, rising to his feet. "Please don't follow me. I don't need a guard."

Caledon dropped his hand. His fingers felt rough and scratchy against his palm now that the silk of dark hair was gone. "If it bothers you I'll stay away," he said quietly. He felt as though he had made a mistake just now and that bothered him. What was it about Hadrian that left him so unsettled?

At the mercenary's capitulation, Hadrian's shoulders sagged slightly with relief. "Thank you."

Caledon tilted his head back once more, his easy smile in place as though it had never left. "You're welcome."

The hint of a shy smile ghosted Hadrian's lips. He moved to leave.

"Please see me tonight, Hadrian."

The younger man's step faltered. More nervous than he liked, Caledon turned to stare at the melting sun that was now but a sliver of gold on the horizon.

"I don't think that's a good idea."

Caledon let the gold fill his eyes. "Please, Hadrian."

He hadn't meant to make it sound so entreating, but the inadvertent honesty worked as a lie might not have.

"Perhaps," Hadrian murmured. He said it quickly, as though needing to say it before his resolve left him.

Caledon watched the sun sink, listening to the other man hurry away. He sighed and closed his eyes. In his heart weighed something he had not felt for many seasons. It was hope. It felt odd.

He'd wasted his coin on supper, Hadrian thought. He should have known better than to try to eat while his stomach churned with anxiety. He hadn't been able to force more than a tiny morsel of bread between his lips before he'd given up the attempt. Ah, well. How was he to know? He'd never felt this way before in his life.

The Fickle Harper Inn was a muted hum behind him. Occasionally the door would open and the loud sounds of conversation and the flute would spill out into the empty street. But mostly it was quiet as Hadrian stood before the doors of the stable; just the tiny rustle of rodents scurrying through the hay and the pounding of his heartbeat, surely the loudest sound in Rhiad.

He didn't know what he was doing here. If his father found out, well... it would be unpleasant. This trip to Rhiad wasn't supposed to be a time for fulfilling personal curiosities no matter how demanding.

But you may never get this chance again.

And that was the reason he was here. Caledon was interested in him. It was so inconceivable to Hadrian that he knew he'd be a fool to pass up this rare opportunity. Not to mention the fact that Hadrian couldn't fight his own attraction for the mercenary. Caledon was the most handsome man he had ever seen. But that didn't completely explain the attraction. There was more to the man. Regret behind the bravado. Caledon had been close to sharing a secret with him and Hadrian had felt special because of that. He wanted to learn more.

Learn more of a carnal nature too. He was aware of the particulars of congress between a man and a woman. But what about between a man and a man? And although he understood the physical mechanics of the act—which made him hot to think of it—he hadn't comprehended the feeling that came with it. Now though, he was beginning to.

It was that wild, fluttery feeling in his stomach. It was the strange surge of blood to his lower body that left him feeling faint and exhilarated at the same time. It wasn't love. He understood that love was an emotion he might never come across in his life. But what he was feeling was something almost as potent. It was lust.

Lust made his hand shake as he pushed the doors aside

and peered into the darkness of the stables. It made his breath short as he slid the doors shut behind him and waited for his eyes to adjust. He was scared. He was excited. It was all he could do not to jump out of his skin when Caledon's voice drifted over him from out of the darkness.

"I was afraid you wouldn't show."

So was I.

A hand found in him the dark, the same calloused palm that had cradled his hand earlier in the day. It now enfolded his own in a familiarity that made Hadrian's cheeks hot. He let himself be led to the end of the stables. At the last stall, Caledon opened the door and gently tugged Hadrian inside. A black mare occupied the stall, snorting softly.

"This is Isaleyn," the mercenary said fondly. "My little girl." Wide cracks in the stable walls allowed enough moonlight inside to highlight Caledon's profile as he leaned in towards his horse. "Isa, love, this is Hadrian."

Caledon brought their hands up and pressed Hadrian's palm to the silky neck of the horse. The mercenary's hand settled atop his.

The feel of the horse was reassuring to Hadrian. When he began stroking her neck Caledon's hand followed him, his larger fingers slipping between Hadrian's. It was oddly intimate but not in a way that left him feeling uneasy. It was simply... pleasant.

"She's lovely," Hadrian murmured, his hand tingling from the contrasts of Isa's cool, sleek hair and Caledon's warm, rough skin. He smiled when Isa swung her head around, a brown eye rolling towards him as if she'd understood the compliment. "How long have you had her?"

"Since she was a filly. She's my baby, aren't you, girl?" The coo of Caledon's voice might have sounded humorous under different circumstances. Hadrian found himself becoming slightly jealous.

"You've taken wonderful care of her," Hadrian said. "She is a prize, truly."

He felt the mercenary shrug. "Yes, well, as much as I love her it wouldn't do for others to see me trying to sneak her into my bed," he said with a grin. "A horse is only good for so much. Then you need to look elsewhere for your company."

This last was said in a lowered voice, close to Hadrian's ear. A tremble in Isa's skin was transmitted through his hand to Caledon's. Or was it the other way around? Hadrian was beginning to grow a little dizzy.

"Is this—is this all you wanted to show me, then?" he asked faintly.

The hand disappeared from atop his. Hadrian shut his eyes, regretting his forwardness. He didn't know how to play this game, obviously. Should he have said nothing and allowed the other man to control the conversation? He didn't know. Yet again, he cursed his ignorance in such matters.

But Caledon hadn't left him. In fact the mercenary was closer than before, pressing up against Hadrian's back. Shocked, Hadrian could only continue to stroke the horse unthinkingly as an arm slid around his waist from behind.

"I'm trying to make you comfortable," Caledon murmured against his ear. Hadrian sucked in his breath as soft lips hummed against the outer shell of his ear. "I know you're inexperienced. I don't want to scare you off by moving too fast. I thought meeting Isa would be a nice start to getting to know me better."

Hadrian summoned up a touch of indignation. "I'm not as green... as green as you think." He tried not to moan when the lips at his ear drifted lower to his neck.

"No?" Caledon smiled against his skin. "Then does that mean someone has done this to you before?" Scorching heat seared the side of Hadrian's neck as Caledon opened his mouth and ran his tongue over Hadrian's skin.

Hadrian nearly jumped out of the other man's arms in

shock. Oh, gods! his frazzled brain cried. What is he doing? But he liked it. Oh, yes. So he forced himself to stammer out a panted, "Y-yes. Of course I've.... oh, of course I've—someone's done that to me."

The heated tip of Caledon's tongue ran a sinuous trail up and down the side of his neck. When it slid down the junction between his neck and shoulder Hadrian's fingers and toes curled. He had to force the digits flat upon Isa's neck. He could feel himself shaking as Caledon continued to lick him. Lick him. By the gods, he'd never imagined anyone doing that to him. It felt so good, that sleek wetness tickling him and yet not. The sheer wetness of Caledon's tongue and its odd firm strength against Hadrian's neck were making the blood drain from his head and fall to his nether parts.

Caledon's breath cooled the moisture on Hadrian's skin. "And I suppose this is nothing new to you either?" Sharp teeth sunk into the flesh of Hadrian's shoulder, right where it met his neck. Hadrian gasped and then bit his lip to cover up the sound.

His vision was going blurry. He tried to concentrate on the sight of his hand, pressed almost desperately against the side of Caledon's horse. Just brush Isa. Brush Isa. He made himself move. Watching his own pale hand stroke up and down the dark hair of the horse helped to ground him somewhat.

"You've done all of this, then?" Caledon asked in a husked whisper.

Oh, but that voice threatened to undo him again. "Yes," Hadrian panted, feeling himself shiver despite the flush of heat that was blazing throughout his body. "All of... gods, all of it."

Caledon's head lifted from Hadrian's neck. The arm around his waist squeezed almost reassuringly, then dropped away. Hadrian's breath hitched with disappointment but Caledon continued to speak, echoing his words with actions.

"So if I turned you around," the mercenary continued to whisper as he gently urged Hadrian to turn to face him, "and pressed you back against my horse, giving you nowhere to run to, nowhere to hide—" his grin showed whitely in the dim lighting, "—you wouldn't fight me because you've done this before." Hadrian stared up at him helplessly, knowing his face was aflame and that he was panting too loudly to disguise it. His body was erect with newfound need and he ached—oh, how he ached.

"Yes," Hadrian whispered breathlessly.

Caledon stepped closer and the space between them vanished. Backed against the unyielding body of the mercenary's horse, Hadrian had nowhere to go. He found he wanted it that way.

Fingertips glided down the side of his cheek. He shut his eyes, trembling and not caring that Caledon would be able to feel it. He tensed in expectation when Caledon leaned forward. But all the mercenary did was rub his roughly stubbled cheek against Hadrian's, letting his breath fan the younger man's ear.

"You're more experienced than I thought."

Hadrian hesitated before finally doing what he'd longed to do since meeting Caledon. He raised his hands in the darkness and lightly grasped the other man's shoulders. Muscles as firm as stone shifted beneath his palms. The touch made his fingers buzz with the need to feel more. But he was afraid. Afraid of what he wanted, afraid of asking for it. Caledon calmly erased his fears. The older man reached up and urged Hadrian's hands behind the back of the mercenary's neck. Hadrian smiled weakly in the darkness. This was so much better. Now he could feel the heat of Caledon's skin and he burned just as Hadrian did.

"Since you've done it all before," Caledon murmured in a low, throaty purr against Hadrian's cheek, "you won't mind if I do this."

And Caledon leaned back and kissed him.

Kissed. Never before in his life and never again would it be like this. Hadrian knew it in his soul. He whimpered, not caring that it revealed his inexperience or his need and desperation. This was magickal. Caledon was kissing him so tenderly... Hadrian had never dreamed it would be so soft, so gentle that it left him in a quivering puddle at the other man's feet. Lips coaxed his own. Utterly trusting, he opened to Caledon, allowing a curious tongue to slip forward and enter his mouth in an intimate joining.

He moaned at the tender invasion, losing the strength to stand. Caledon caught him, pressing him back against Isa. Even the great horse's immense heartbeat could not drown out the one stampeding wildly in Hadrian's chest. His senses spun. He could hardly breathe. It was almost frightening how quickly and completely he was losing control of his body and yet it was exciting. To give in to Caledon's knowledgeable caresses, to surrender himself to the other man's confidence, knowing that he was being led to a wondrous place... Never let this end, Hadrian thought dizzily. Never.

Caledon's tongue stroked over his own. It pumped across that wet flesh in an elemental rhythm that made Hadrian tighten his legs around a raging, pulsing need. Timidly, Hadrian let his tongue entangle with the other man's and at his first tentative foray Caledon moaned into his mouth. Hadrian nearly exploded at the sound. Caledon's passion. For him. Because of him. Hadrian's own moan eclipsed the other man's as he clutched helplessly at the back of Caledon's neck. He was so weak he feared he might collapse.

Caledon's mouth tore away from his to whisper, "Breathe, love. Breathe. I've got you." The hands around Hadrian's waist stroked him comfortingly. "You're doing fine, Hadrian. You're beautiful... so beautiful like this."

"Oh, Caledon," Hadrian panted. "I've never—this is..." He couldn't finish the thought. There were no words to describe what he felt.

"I know, love, gods do I know." Caledon made a sound that to Hadrian's muddled senses sounded like quiet laughter. "Who would've believed it'd be like this, eh?" So low Hadrian almost missed it, the mercenary breathed, "Who could've guessed?"

Then he was back to kissing Hadrian again and there was no room left in Hadrian's consciousness for anything else. He held Caledon more boldly now, urging their mouths to mate more tightly. He wanted to climb into Caledon. He wanted to merge with the mercenary so that all Hadrian felt for the rest of his life was this.

All of the blood, all of the nerves in Hadrian's body collected in his mouth and in his groin. He didn't think it could get any better. It was impossible. But Caledon proved him wrong. One of the mercenary's hands slid from around his back. Hadrian was suddenly as sharply aware of the placement of that hand as he would have been a knife at his throat. As Caledon continued to plunder Hadrian's mouth, the mercenary's hand slid down the front of Hadrian's stomach. Hadrian opened his eyes. His breath stuttered. He suddenly knew another way in which this could be better. But would Caledon dare?

He would. Hadrian cried out against the other man's lips when a hot palm cupped him through his breeches. Skilled fingers curled around his swollen length, making Hadrian push forward mindlessly, moaning. Oh, gods, oh, gods, oh, gods. He clenched his eyes shut, no longer able to kiss Caledon back as passion flooded his system. Caledon rubbed him through the cloth, making him grow hotter, harder, until Hadrian was only standing because Caledon held him up.

"That's it, Hadrian. Let go for me. Feel it."

I could die right now.

It was becoming too much. Caledon was kissing his slack lips, murmuring endearments. Hadrian thought his entire body might burst from the too-powerful sensations drowning him. It was beginning to resemble pain. Then

Caledon pulled his hand away.

"No..." Hadrian gasped, opening his eyes.

Caledon smiled down at him, looking pleased. But Hadrian found slight comfort in the mercenary's swift breathing. "I need to slow you down, Hadrian. You're like a wild horse running loose." Caledon bent and brushed his lips over Hadrian's. "But don't worry. I'm more than up to the challenge of taming you. We've a long night ahead of us, love. This is only the beginning."

Hadrian shuddered at the words. He let his eyes drift shut as Caledon met his mouth again. Only the beginning. Even if Caledon's words failed to be true it wouldn't matter. Caledon had already shown him enough wonders to last his lifetime. In the darkness of the stables, with the aromas of hay and horse sharpening his senses and Isa chuffing softly behind him, Hadrian returned Caledon's kiss eagerly. He would never forget this night, he vowed. When he returned to Shard's Point Isle and found himself once again walking the cold, somber halls of the castle, he would pull out this memory and relive it. Because tonight Caledon had shown him that there was another means of summoning magick beyond that which he had been taught. There was the magick to be found in a kiss.

CHAPTER THREE

He could see now that he had erred when he had first tried to label Hadrian.

Caledon had been fascinated by the other man's apparent inexperience, his naiveté. But the truth of the matter was that Hadrian was untouched—untouched by affection, untouched by desire. How this had come to be, Caledon couldn't imagine. But he knew it to be true. He felt it in his bones.

Nothing else could explain why Hadrian literally melted beneath his caresses. Every touch Caledon made upon the younger man's skin left Hadrian trembling and breathless, his body both afraid of the sensation and straining for more. Why has no one done this before me? Caledon wondered as he eased open the stall door with his free arm wrapped firmly about Hadrian's back.

He should simply be grateful that it was he who had been the one to find Hadrian first. That's what his sensible side told him. But a deeper part of him felt unexplainably saddened by the discovery. Everyone deserved the comforts of touch, of affection. Why hadn't anyone offered these things to Hadrian?

Caledon's body urged him to forget such ruminations. He wasn't trying to develop a permanent relationship with the other man. Hadrian would be gone within the week. This would be but an interlude for them both. Even so,

Caledon vowed to make it something worth remembering.

He had managed to back Hadrian to the shaky ladder that led to the loft, but now necessity required that he break off the kiss that was currently stealing his breath. For someone who was being taught the basics minute by minute, Hadrian was proving to be an admirably quick learner. Caledon wasn't surprised. Within the swirling grey depths of Hadrian's eyes lurked a passion that did not know itself. All it needed was an introduction.

He regretfully eased out of the kiss and cupped Hadrian's chin, tilting his face up. Caledon nearly groaned with desire for the other man. With cheeks flushed like cherry wine and dark lashes shuttering the mysterious silver of his gaze, Hadrian was a temptation few would be able to resist. Looking down at him, Caledon wondered why he was trying. Oh, yes. The loft.

"Will you come with me up into the loft?" he asked gently. This was an important turning point and he didn't want to scare the younger man off.

Hadrian blinked as though trying to clear a fog from his vision. "The loft?" he repeated, uncomprehending.

"I've a blanket up there," Caledon explained, feeling a bit of a lecher as he admitted to having anticipated Hadrian's company. "We can relax and look up at the stars."

"Alright," Hadrian agreed after a moment.

He has no idea, Caledon thought. But he noticed that Hadrian's hand on the ladder was less than steady as he pulled himself up. Did he suspect after all?

With sweating hands and a pulse that roared beneath his skin, Caledon followed Hadrian up the ladder. True to his word, Caledon had laid a thick blanket over the scratchy mounds of hay, providing them with a more comfortable place to recline. He recognized the self-consciousness that made Hadrian's movements stiff as he dropped onto the blanket. The wave of tenderness that swept through Caledon was a surprise to him.

He'd placed the blanket before the large opening in the stable wall where new hay was brought up from the outside. It provided them with a portrait-like framed view of the town stretched before them and of the night sky twinkling above.

"This is... very nice," Hadrian said quietly. He turned from admiring the view outside, his eyes going suddenly round as he looked up at Caledon.

The mercenary smiled as he stripped off his tunic and let it drop to the straw. He could tell that Hadrian didn't want to look but his willpower was weak. Grey eyes swept hungrily, curiously, across his chest and down the flat plane of his abdomen. Like what you see, Hadrian? The quick flick of a tongue across rosy lips said that he did.

Still watching the younger man's reaction, Caledon let his hands fall to the ties of his breeches. He hesitated for half a beat, waiting to see if Hadrian would protest this sudden escalation of their intimacy. Though he blushed furiously and his hands curled into fists upon his thighs, Hadrian said nothing, eyes riveted almost helplessly to the mercenary's hands.

Hadrian wanted him so badly he didn't know how to say it. The thought made Caledon grow harder with need. It made things a bit more difficult when it came time to drawing his breeches down over his hips. There was a significant... protuberance he had to overcome first. But once past his hips he swiftly stripped the garment off, drawing his boots long with it.

"This is what you do to me," Caledon said in a voice not his own. Hadrian's eyes darted to the mercenary's eyes then back to the proudly arcing flesh that rose from between his thighs. Already reddened cheeks grew brighter with color. "My body finds you desirable, Hadrian. It wants to find pleasure with you. Can you understand that?"

Hesitantly, Hadrian nodded. "I can. I-I feel that way about you as well. Only, I don't know how to... how to answer that need."

Caledon savored the younger man's answer. It made him smile as he dropped to one knee on the blanket beside Hadrian. It faded somewhat when Hadrian shied away at his approach.

"It's alright. You may touch me."

With a visible gathering of nerves, Hadrian leaned forward, reaching out to touch Caledon's bare chest. The mercenary bit back a groan as slender fingers delicately explored his skin.

"You are scarred," Hadrian breathed, frowning slightly as though he thought Caledon still pained by the marks.

"I am a mercenary," Caledon reminded him, reaching up himself to thread his fingers through the other man's dark hair. He pushed his hand to the back of Hadrian's head and urged him to look up. "Will you do something with me?"

The other man nodded wordlessly.

"I want you to play a game with me," Caledon began, gently caressing Hadrian's scalp. "When I touch myself I want you to do the same to your body. Will you do that for me?"

Hadrian wavered between looking mortified and intrigued. "You want me to touch myself. For you?"

Caledon nodded. "This way we can both see each other and learn what brings the other pleasure." He leaned forward and pressed a kiss to the corner of Hadrian's mouth, feeling the lips part for him automatically. "Please, Hadrian?" He took a pale hand and pressed it to his own chest, sliding it over the hard pebble of a nipple. When the hand trembled within his grip he slid it lower, down his stomach to rest on the taut skin just below his navel. "Please?"

Hadrian was panting against his cheek. "I suppose I can... do that."

Caledon held back his smile as Hadrian sat up and turned himself slightly away from the mercenary. Glancing back over his shoulder as if to be certain the blond wouldn't pounce on him, Hadrian fumbled with the broach on his cloak, finally managing to remove it. Caledon tugged the cloak away and tossed it to the growing pile of garments.

"Now the tunic," he urged softly.

Hadrian took an audible breath before pulling the thick cloth up his chest and over his head. Caledon sighed in contentment. Hadrian was as beautiful as he'd imagined. Pale, porcelain skin covered a slender musculature that hinted at a lean strength. Hadrian wasn't power, he was all grace and sleek curves. Caledon appreciated the physique with a connoisseur's eye for beauty.

"I'm not like you," Hadrian was saying, eyeing the mercenary nervously. "I'm not strong like you or—"

"I'm glad," Caledon interrupted. "I don't want you to be those things. I want you to be just as you are. We fit together better this way." A faint, grateful smile touched the corners of Hadrian's mouth. Caledon returned it. "Keep going, Hadrian. You're doing fine."

Nodding, once again nervous, Hadrian plucked at the ties on his breeches. Anticipation was killing Caledon but he forced his expression to be one of patient understanding. His body couldn't say the same. By the time Hadrian had managed to wiggle his way out of his breeches and shove it and his boots to the straw at their feet, Caledon's flesh was rock hard and weeping with need. A brief glimpse of pale, tightly rounded buttocks made him swallow back a moan. As for his view of the other—

"Move your hand, love," he gently coaxed. "Everything I've seen of you is beautiful. You don't need to hide."

Staring up at the rafters with his lips pinched tightly, Hadrian dropped his hand to the blanket. Moonlight slanted over his body, caressing the slender column of ivory flesh that curved outward from within a dark shadow. The tip of that smooth flesh glistened with the proof of Hadrian's excitement. He was not as large as the mercenary but he was stunning in his pale beauty. Caledon unconsciously licked his lips, amazed that he hadn't already thrown himself atop the younger man.

"Oh, love," he breathed, shifting restlessly on the blanket. "You had nothing to worry about. You're perfect."

Skeptical grey eyes slid to him.

"You're exactly what I want," Caledon assured him. He gave a self-effacing laugh. "In fact, you're more than I expected. I may have to cut my game short."

Something that looked like hope, which tore Caledon's insides to see, sparked in Hadrian's eyes. "You find me attractive, then? You still want to... be with me?"

"Mmm, let me show you how much." Moving more quickly than he knew he should but unable to restrain himself any longer now that Hadrian lay naked before him, Caledon brushed the back of his fingers across the younger man's collarbones. It was a light, barely-there touch but Hadrian shut his eyes and sighed, his head falling back slightly.

Encouraged by the response, Caledon's hand floated lower, grazing a small, strawberry-tinted nipple. This time Hadrian's eyes shot open, his lips parting in surprise as Caledon lightly pinched the tiny nub. Caledon noted the gratifying reaction lower down Hadrian's body.

"Did that feel good?" he whispered.

Hadrian nodded, gripping the blanket. "Do it again. Please."

Grinning, Caledon turned his attention to the other nipple and circled the aureole with a fingertip. Round and round he circled, watching the flesh pucker up in agitation. Before Hadrian could guess at his intent Caledon swooped down and sucked the nipple between his lips.

Slender fingers grasped Caledon's hair as a shocked cry reverberated through the loft. This one likes to make noise, he thought with satisfaction. Nice. He sucked the pebble of flesh and rolled it across his tongue. He could feel movement on the blanket and knew without looking that Hadrian was already moving his hips, blindly searching. So quick, so eager. Caledon's body was hot with anticipation.

When he finally raised his head, satisfied that he had left Hadrian's skin sensitive to the touch, the younger man was looking at him with bright, silver eyes. "May I touch you too?" Hadrian asked with an excitement that made his voice sound breathy and light.

"I'd like nothing better," Caledon replied. He waited, curious to see how Hadrian would touch him, and nearly exploded when slender fingers lightly stroked his erection. "Gods, Hadrian, you're bold!"

The fingers immediately withdrew, Hadrian's cheeks pale. "I'm sorry!"

Caledon caught his wrist. "No," he said hoarsely, "don't stop. This is more than I was hoping for; don't tease me by drawing away now."

Swallowing hard, Hadrian allowed the mercenary to return his hand to the stiff flesh jutting out from between Caledon's thighs. Caledon let his eyelids fall nearly shut as hesitant hands gingerly explored him from base to tip. This was torture, it truly was, but Caledon would sooner impale himself on his own blade than discourage Hadrian from what he was doing. It was just enough sensation to make his flesh lengthen and harden further. It was light enough to leave Caledon all but twisting on the blanket in need of more. When the soft caresses grew too much to endure, he reached between their bodies and took careful hold of Hadrian's erection.

The reaction was instant and exactly what Caledon had hoped for. Hadrian's eyes rolled up into his head, his hands falling slack to the blanket as he collapsed backwards. A red flush drifted up his throat and lingered on his cheeks as he lay gasping for breath and unable to find it. Caledon leaned over him, stroking him firmly, introducing the younger man to the wonders of another's hand upon that most intimate flesh.

"It feels better like this, doesn't it?" he murmured, watching from beneath his lashes as Hadrian writhed beneath him. Pale, slender thighs fell open on the blanket in unconscious offering and Caledon had to fight the nearly violent urge to dive between those slim thighs and push himself into the tight body with all his might.

But he couldn't do that, not even if Hadrian by some miracle begged it of him. Caledon forced himself to remember who this was beneath him. His untouched jewel of Rhiad. He wouldn't dare crack its surface with so barbaric a joining. This one required a bit of finesse. Caledon could only hope he had the fortitude for the job.

"Hadrian, love," he murmured, burying his face in the spill of dark hair that lay across pale shoulders, "do you want me to show you more?"

Blind eyes opened with effort. "More?"

"There are ways for men to find pleasure with each other besides this." Caledon rubbed his thumb across the slick tip of Hadrian's erection, simply so he could watch the other shudder. "I promise you it feels much, much better than what we've done thus far."

Hadrian blinked. "How is that possible?"

Caledon laughed with genuine delight. "Gods, Hadrian, you've a skill for stroking a man's ego. It is no wonder I've fallen so hard for you."

Hadrian's face registered the words at the same moment Caledon realized what he'd said. "You've fallen—"

Caledon squeezed Hadrian's shaft, drawing a desperate moan from the younger man. "Enough," Caledon whispered, shaky for reasons he did not want to think about. "Will you let me show you these things? Will you let me show you the pleasure you and I can find with each other?"

If Hadrian still considered what the mercenary had said, he made no show of it. On his face now was only pure, untarnished lust. "Show me," he breathed. "I want to learn everything."

Caledon smiled, joy and desire unfurling through his body. "Then up onto your knees, love."

Hadrian gathered his shaking limbs beneath him, rising onto all fours. His back trembled beneath Caledon's palm as the mercenary soothed him with long slow strokes up and down his spine.

"You're doing fine, Hadrian. Just fine," he murmured, placing gentle kisses against the back of the younger man's shoulders. "It's going to get a little more intense from here on out but I promise you that you'll like it."

"It's alright," Hadrian panted, his head concealed by the lush fall of his dark hair. "I know you won't hurt me."

Caledon's hand faltered slightly. So trusting. What had he done to make the other man say such a thing? They hardly knew each other. But as he studied Hadrian's faintly trembling body, Caledon knew that the younger man was caught in the throes of his passion, willing to do anything for more.

So responsive... Caledon's body hardened further. Anything he did to Hadrian this night would push the younger man into ecstasy. Hadrian's pleasure would be so easy to manipulate. Caledon's pulse quickened at the prospect.

He stroked both of his palms up and down the pale back before him, using the touch to soothe and relax. Hadrian was tense, still nervous about what would happen yet eager to find out. Thinking too much, Caledon decided. That needed to end.

He reached up and ran his fingers through Hadrian's hair, letting the silky strands slip between the webbing. He gently massaged the bent head, earning a sensual groan as Caledon expertly found all the points on the other man's scalp that would set his entire head to tingling. Hadrian moaned, looking ready to collapse back onto the blanket. Caledon smiled and slid his hands down over the back of Hadrian's neck and began to knead the tight muscles.

"You need to relax, love," he murmured. "This is only going to feel good. Just take it easy."

"I'm sorry," Hadrian panted. "I'm trying..."

"Shhh, don't apologize." Caledon lightly bit a sleekly muscled shoulder. "Don't think about anything except how this feels. Forget your mind, Hadrian. Become your body. Feel what I'm doing to you. Enjoy it."

After a moment of hard kneading, Caledon felt the muscles ease beneath his hands. "That's it." He continued the massage lower, working out the tight knots of Hadrian's shoulders and once they were soft and warm, down along the muscles bracketing his spine.

In the moonlight, Hadrian's skin glowed. Caledon's ministrations became less massage and more caressing as he drifted down the graceful curve of the younger man's body. At the swell of his hips, Caledon settled his palms over the creamy globes of Hadrian's buttocks and gently squeezed. Hadrian made a low sound and pushed back ever so slightly. Caledon palmed the soft flesh, satisfying his need to mold Hadrian's buttocks to the shape of his hands. He spread the pale flesh slightly, glimpsing the tiny pink entrance his body yearned for. The mercenary laughed quietly to himself at how his shaft jumped with excitement at the sight. I need to heed my own advice and calm down, he mused.

Hadrian heard the laugh and lifted his head. Silver-grey eyes flashed over his shoulder. "What are you—what are you laughing about?"

Even in the milky light, Caledon could see that the younger man's cheeks were flushed red with arousal and mounting embarrassment.

"Don't even think that I'm laughing at you," Caledon told him with quiet sternness. "It is I whom I am poking fun at. I see your lovely body and I feel myself losing control. I am ashamed at how green my body is acting."

The grey eyes regarded him steadily. "Is it so bad to be... green?"

The whispered question pinched Caledon's heart. He moved up over Hadrian's body, draping an arm around his waist while one hand braced against the straw. "Is it so bad that I get to be the first to show you pleasure?" he whispered into a pale ear. "Is it so bad that I get to be the first to hear you moan in desire, the first to brand my touch onto your skin... is that what you mean?" He felt Hadrian shiver beneath him. "Oh, no, Hadrian. Being green is good. Being green makes me hard." As proof, he rubbed himself against the curve of a buttock, letting Hadrian feel how true his words were.

Hadrian let out a ragged sigh. "Caledon. Keep going."

Caledon smiled and dragged his tongue along the swell of a shoulder as the fingers of one hand drifted across Hadrian's chest, searching. He caught a tiny nipple and gently rolled it between his fingertips. Hadrian bucked beneath him, unconsciously rolling his hips in a way that left Caledon's mouth dry. Gods, but Hadrian was sensual without even knowing that he was. He was like a horse that yearned for the freedom of the open range and yet desired a strong hand to guide him there. Let it be me.

Caledon continued to play with the small nub of flesh, relishing the sounds Hadrian made against his chest. He found Hadrian's other nipple and played with it until it too, was sensitive to just the tiniest of brushes of his fingertips. He began to kiss his way down Hadrian's back, mirroring the motion with his hand beneath until his fingers circled the indentation of Hadrian's navel. He felt the inhalation of breath more than he heard it.

"I'm going to touch you," Caledon told him in a husky voice. "Would you like that?"

Hadrian made a sound and Caledon knew that he must be biting his lip.

"Would you like me to stroke that ache between your thighs?" he teased. "Do you remember how good it felt to have my hand wrapped around you, squeezing you, stroking you—"

"Please!" Hadrian gasped, thrusting against air. "Please do it."

Caledon couldn't help himself, aroused by the novelty of having someone so innocent beneath him. "Please, what, Hadrian? Say it."

"T-touch me!"

Caledon shut his eyes, thrilled by the spark of fire that ripped through his veins. "Hadrian, you're going to kill me before this is over," he said with a breathy laugh. "Let me return the favor."

He curled his fingers about the hard heat that jutted up from Hadrian's thighs, grinning into the darkness as Hadrian cried out, his head flying back.

"Have you ever had anyone touch you this way?" he asked as he stroked the velvety flesh in his palm.

"N-never before you!" Hadrian gasped, twisting and writhing in and out of Caledon's hand as if he didn't know how to move. "Oh, gods, Caledon—it feels so good."

"It gets better, love."

He pumped Hadrian steadily, listening to his breathing become faster, more desperate. Caledon read the signs of his growing passion in the uncontrollable jerking of his hips, the clenching of his fists in the blanket. His moans filled the otherwise silent night. Hadrian was so excited it stole Caledon's breath. It also gave him pause. Hadrian should have found release by now, but somehow he hadn't.

"Don't fight it," Caledon told him, reaching down to cradle the twin globes behind the shaft he fisted. The added sensation made Hadrian release a desperate moan. "Why are you holding on?" he asked in a soft voice. "It's alright to let go. It's only you and me here. It's alright, Hadrian. Don't be afraid."

"Caledon... please," Hadrian whimpered.

Caledon didn't know what he was asking for. For him to stop? For him to continue? It could have been either. Caledon had never had anyone fight their desires this way.

It was alarming and enflaming at the same time. His own cock grew harder at the visible and audible signs of Hadrian's resistance. Caledon couldn't help himself from rubbing himself against a slender thigh.

"What is it you want?" he asked the quaking body beneath him. "What do you need?"

Hadrian shook his head frantically. He was so swollen in Caledon's hand that the mercenary knew it must be nearing pain. "Just... hold—"

He didn't finish but Caledon understood. With a strong arm wrapped about Hadrian's waist, he lifted the younger man upright and held him against his chest. Hadrian collapsed back into his embrace, his head falling to the side so that his breath flashed across Caledon's collarbone.

"I've got you," Caledon breathed, beginning to ache himself. "Just let go. I won't let you fall."

With a broken cry, Hadrian arched against him, fingers digging painfully into the arm wrapped about his waist. Caledon breathed a sigh of relief as warmth dripped down his fingers and Hadrian became boneless within his arms. Hadrian made a sound very similar to a sob and dropped his head against Caledon's shoulder.

Caledon's breath fanned his hair as he looked down at the spent man. "You fought that the entire time, you beautiful fool. I'd no idea you were into self-torture. Perhaps I'll tie you up next time, eh?" He grinned into the dazed grey eyes that looked up at him in confusion. "Never mind. I was joking."

Hadrian shifted, his eyes clearing as Caledon's erection jabbed into the small of his back. "Caledon?"

"That was just the beginning," the mercenary told him in a thickening voice. "Now comes the truly wild part." He kissed Hadrian's lips and murmured against the soft skin, "Back down, love. I want to show you something."

Hesitantly, Hadrian bent forward again. Caledon spent a moment admiring his sweat-sheened body with hands and eyes. Hadrian responded immediately to his touches, his skin sensitized and reacting to the slightest touch. He moaned softly as Caledon caressed him into hardness once again.

"So beautiful," Caledon murmured, stroking him leisurely. With his free hand, he reached beneath the blanket and dug around in the straw. He grinned when he found the small pot of salve he had secreted there earlier. Arrogant? Perhaps. Willing to be caught unprepared? Never.

Coating the tips of his fingers with the sweet-smelling salve, he let his fingers float over the curves of Hadrian's hips. Hadrian was fully hard now, moving somewhat fitfully in Caledon's hand.

"Eager like a colt," Caledon teased, earning him a dark look from over Hadrian's shoulder.

"Don't compare me to livestock," the other man protested. "Even though you're about to... about to..." He couldn't say it, suddenly ducking his head.

"Even though I'm about to take you," Caledon finished for him, choosing kinder words than he knew the other was thinking. "Don't worry, Hadrian. I've no doubt in my mind that all of this lovely skin and the exquisite limbs they cover belong solely to the beautiful young man I met yesterday. No doubt at all who it is I'm with. I'm grateful."

Hadrian trembled, whether at the words or Caledon's fingers currently tracing the crease between his buttocks, the mercenary had no idea. Watching the younger man intently from beneath lowered lids, Caledon found the puckered entrance to Hadrian's body and lightly circled it. Hadrian shifted restlessly, perturbed by the unfamiliar touch.

"Relax," Caledon purred, rubbing his fingertip over the clenching muscle. "This will feel good. I promise you. But you need to relax first, and let me in." Caledon picked up the speed of his strokes along Hadrian's shaft and used the distraction to push the tip of his finger inside. "There you go. Easy."

"I don't know if I like this," Hadrian panted. "It feels odd." His body belied his words though, as it pushed back ever so slightly upon the invading digit.

"It's going to feel damned good in a minute," Caledon assured him. "Just wait. I'll have you in a quivering puddle in no time."

Hadrian laughed tensely. "And that's a good thing?"

Caledon smiled as he twisted his finger, drawing a startled gasp from his young lover. "Oh, yes, Hadrian. That's a very good thing. You'll see."

With watchful eyes that knew what to look for, Caledon stroked over that nub of pleasure. Hadrian's body reacted to the sudden influx of pleasure with a suddenness that nearly jerked him off of Caledon's fingers. Caledon caught the bucking body tighter about the waist, holding Hadrian steady as he explored the tight passage, unerringly hitting that spot again and again.

Hadrian released a shuddery moan, caught between the twin pleasures of Caledon's hands on his shaft and in his body. Caledon felt the constricting muscles about his finger release slightly and took that as a signal to go further. He carefully slid another finger inside and then another, pumping them into the loosening channel of Hadrian's body.

"How does that feel?" the mercenary panted, placing an openmouthed kiss against the back of the other man's shoulder. "Do you like what I'm doing to you?"

Hadrian moaned, his arms nearly dropping him to the blanket as Caledon relentlessly stroked him, inside and out. "I can't... stand it," he gasped. "Don't stop."

Caledon chuckled. "What if I stopped only to put something bigger here." He pressed his fingers down, making Hadrian spread his legs and roll his hips in unconscious need. "Something bigger, and harder and hotter rubbing right over this." He nipped a pale shoulder. "Would you like that, love? Hmm?"

Hadrian's hands tore at the blanket. His body was slick

and shiny with the force of his desire. Shudders periodically traveled up the length of his body, the shivers transmitted to Caledon's chest and arm. Caledon knew he was so close. He just needs a little push.

"Would you like me to fill you up?" he continued in a husky voice, his own hips starting to move with barely restrained need. "Would you like me to push into you and ease that ache you have, Hadrian? I bet you ache. I bet it feels so good it almost hurts."

He knew the purr of his voice would get to Hadrian. The younger man responded electrically to all of his prompts. This time was no different. Hadrian pushed himself backwards, impaling himself on Caledon's fingers desperately.

"What do you want?" Caledon whispered. "Tell me."

Hadrian panted. "You know what I want."

"But I want to hear you ask me for it."

Hadrian made a strangled sound of frustration. "You're being cruel!"

Caledon grinned in the dark, pumping his hands steadily to push the other man closer to his limit. "I never said I was a nice man, love. Just tell me what you want. I want to hear your innocent mouth say the words. Tell me."

"Unnh... Caledon—"

He leaned forward to catch the whispered words. "Yes?"

"—take me. Please."

Caledon groaned, his cock too hard to deny its pleasure any longer. He removed his fingers from the loosened passage and positioned himself in their place. So slowly it made him clench his teeth with the struggle for control, he pushed the head of his shaft past the tight ring of muscle. From somewhere far away he heard Hadrian give a small cry. Instinct prompted Caledon to stroke the flesh he still held beneath Hadrian's body. Hadrian jerked, inadvertently pushing the mercenary deeper into him. Hadrian stilled, his body shaking as Caledon eased himself in the last few inches.

Ah, gods, tight. Caledon could think of nothing else but the silken fist of Hadrian's body squeezing him almost painfully. It was a tightness that Caledon knew from experience meant Hadrian hadn't fully accepted him. Sweating, his nerves stretched to the breaking point, Caledon nonetheless took the time to gently stroke the quivering body beneath him.

"Easy, Hadrian, easy," he soothed in a rough voice. "I'm inside now. It won't become worse than this; it will only get better."

"Caledon," the other whispered raggedly. Hadrian was breathing quickly, his chest heaving. "I feel so full... I can't take so much."

Caledon bit his tongue, his flesh swelling even more at the unintentionally erotic words. He swore to himself when Hadrian hissed in response to his growing ardor. This wasn't getting better for either of them. Caledon decided quickly that it was time to change that.

Hadrian's erection had softened in his palm, but with careful kneading and squeezing Caledon swiftly brought him back to full hardness. The return of pleasure had an added benefit for Hadrian's body as well, helping it to relax. Caledon sighed in relief when he felt the tight constriction about his flesh loosen somewhat. Now it was up to him.

He pulled back slightly, letting himself ease from Hadrian's body. Then he slowly pushed back in. He angled himself purposefully and was rewarded for his efforts when Hadrian let out a long, low moan, his back arching like a cat's.

Caledon grinned at the reaction. "Oh, yes, that's it. Show me that again, Hadrian."

He slid out with the same maddening pace and eased back in. He almost laughed when Hadrian mimicked the exact response as before. "Oh, you're beautiful," Caledon marveled. "Look at you. So sensitive..."

He began to thrust carefully now, making sure to strike that place of pleasure inside Hadrian's body with every stroke. Hadrian's moans turned into full-throated groans of pleasure. He twisted beneath Caledon, his cock stiff and weeping in the mercenary's hand. Caledon could not remember ever seeing anything so breathtaking—so carnal and yet so pure. Someone like Hadrian shouldn't exist and yet he did, and Caledon had been the first to find him. What have I done, Caledon thought in amazement, that allows me to deserve this?

Hadrian was fiery heat about his pumping shaft. Every thrust was like pushing himself into a fire-warmed glove. Caledon thrust in a little harder now, allowing more of his passion for the lithe body to be appeased. This only stirred Hadrian to be more vocal, his moans echoing off the rafters. Caledon was in ecstasy.

With a growl, he released Hadrian's erection and grabbed the slighter man about the hips. Hadrian's body accepted him completely now. Caledon knew that the rough thrusts with which he now took the other man wouldn't hurt. If anything Hadrian enjoyed it more, his arms collapsing to the blanket with only the mercenary's hands to hold him up. Caledon pumped into him furiously, grinding himself tight against the pale curve of buttocks to reach as deep as he could.

But it wasn't enough somehow and he thought he knew what was missing. Hadrian let out a surprised yelp as Caledon expertly flipped the younger man onto his back, never losing their intimate contact. Wide, grey eyes looked up in surprise from beneath a swirling mass of inky hair. With the moonlight pouring down from the opened window, Caledon could see the splash of rosy color that infused Hadrian's cheeks. Hadrian looked wild and wanton and in the process of being thoroughly tumbled. Caledon grinned. This was exactly what he wanted.

Enjoying Hadrian's mixed expression of confusion and passion, Caledon hooked a pale leg over one shoulder and leaned forward, driving himself deeper into the body pinned below. The grey eyes went impossibly wide. Raven-black lashes fluttered down weakly. Still smiling, Caledon reached between their bodies and took hold of Hadrian's erection again and began to pump it.

"Better?" he breathed.

When the grey eyes opened again they glimmered in the moonlight. Tears? Caledon was afraid to look too closely. So he shut his own eyes and gave himself over to the task of driving Hadrian insensate with pleasure. His long, deep thrusts left Hadrian clutching at Caledon's shoulders and gasping. He began to move with Caledon, small shifts of his hips at first and then more determined thrusts as his confidence grew. To the mercenary, it was like watching a tightly budded flower open and bloom.

"Hadrian," he whispered. There was more in his voice than even he expected to hear.

A little afraid, a little desperate, Caledon bore down on the slender body beneath his. He lifted Hadrian's leg higher and angled himself carefully. He began to make short, hard jabs directly against the center of Hadrian's pleasure. Hadrian let out a strangled cry, his head arching back against the blanket. His nails dug into Caledon's skin painfully. The mercenary knew this was the end for them both and began to piston faster.

Hadrian's voice grew hoarse with his short cries. Caledon had never heard anyone lose their voice while in the throes of their passion. It left his mouth dry, his heart a stampeding pain in his chest. Not thinking at all, controlled by forces he couldn't name, he leaned forward and muffled Hadrian's cries with his mouth. With his eyes open, he watched the grey eyes stare back at him in shock. Then blackness swept down to hide them as Hadrian gave a final groan and shuddered beneath Caledon.

The heat of Hadrian's essence damped the mercenary's hand at the same time his own release ripped through him. His body jerked with each powerful jet into the trembling body surrounding him. Caledon felt as though he'd been trampled by a hundred horses and yet something inside of him felt inexplicably light, as though it soared beyond his body. He didn't want to know what that strange feeling meant. It was enough that he had just had the most incredible physical experience in recent memory. It was more than enough.

"Caledon." He felt trembling fingers stroke his sweat-dampened hair from his temples. Groaning, he dropped to the blanket beside Hadrian, regretfully leaving the younger man's clenching heat.

He turned his leaden head and found those crystalline eyes gazing at him with almost drunken pleasure. "What is it, love?"

"Is it—is it always like that? I had no idea."

Caledon grinned ruefully, staring up through the opening in the roof at the shifting swathe of milky stars. "No, actually, it's rarely like that. I can't explain why this was different." *I don't want to.*

Hadrian gave a soft, disappointed, "Oh." Minutes passed in which their breathing eased and grew synchronized. Caledon shifted and threw a heavy leg across the top of Hadrian's thighs, one arm sliding beneath the spill of dark hair to urge Hadrian closer. *Possessive!,* a voice inside him accused. At the moment, Caledon was too content to care.

"Do you think it will be that way between us again?"

Caledon blinked at the unexpected question, a slow grin curving his lips. He stroked the dark hair fanned across his chest. "Yes, Hadrian, I think it will. In fact why don't we find out?"

Hadrian's startled moan was caught by Caledon's lips. "So soon?"

Caledon kissed him silent. "So soon."

Caledon waited in the shadow of the stable doors as Hadrian pulled his cloak about him.

"I'll see you tomorrow, won't I?" Hadrian asked, a touch of worry shading his voice.

He had small bits of straw in his hair and his tunic was rumpled and bunched about the waist but Caledon didn't point out these things. Hadrian looked freshly tumbled and Caledon wanted all of Rhiad to see and wonder who was responsible.

"Of course. Don't think I'll let you get away from me that easily, love. There's much more I need to teach you."

Hadrian blushed. "Surely there can't be much—"

"There is," Caledon told him with a smirk. "Trust me." His fingers graced a high cheekbone. "I intend to give you a very thorough education, love."

Hadrian smiled at him, catching the mercenary's hand. "I like it when you call me that."

Caledon looked at him. I enjoy using it to describe you. He pulled his hand back regretfully. "Go now. You need your rest. I'll see you on the morrow."

Hadrian hesitated before darting forward and placing a quick, soft kiss against the mercenary's lips. He laughed quietly at Caledon's expression before slipping away onto the street. Caledon stared after him, fighting the urge to follow to be sure no one harassed the younger man. When Hadrian had rounded the corner and disappeared from sight, Caledon raised a hand to touch his lips.

"Who was that pretty piece of flesh?" said a mocking voice from the street.

Caledon dropped his hand, instinctively reaching for a weapon. He relaxed when he saw the two slender young men watching him with matching grins on their faces. "Gam. Lio," he greeted the one-eyed thieves. He looked at them suspiciously. "What brings you two around the stables?"

The scarred thief with the hazel eye shrugged innocently. "Oh, nothing much," Gam said. "Lio and I heard noises up in the loft and thought we'd investigate." His lips quivered with the grin that didn't quite fully form. "Sounded alarmingly intense, it did. We were afraid someone was being attacked."

"Guess we were right," his green-eyed companion added dryly. The emerald gaze flicked down the path that Hadrian had taken. "Who was that? I've never seen his like in Rhiad before."

Caledon grinned, allowing a certain degree of smugness to seep into his smile. "You never have and never will. He's my latest obsession and one no one will have the chance to experience him besides me."

Gam and Lio exchanged looks. "Sounds serious," Gam remarked.

Caledon looked after his young lover. "Unfortunately, it can't be. He's leaving in a few days." He shrugged, making light of his disappointment for his friends' sake. Inside though, the reminder that Hadrian would soon be gone was a pain he hadn't anticipated.

He would just have to accept the job Hadrian's father was offering, Caledon decided. It was a way to remain close to Hadrian outside of Rhiad. It would also be an opportunity to find out if maybe, just maybe, Caledon ni Agthon had a chance for something more.

CHAPTER FOUR

He had one more day left in this city that Hadrian had begun to think of as the most beautiful place in the world. Just one more day. It was not enough.

He had spoken with as many mercenaries as he expected to find in Rhiad. It had taken some effort to meet them all. But he had done it. He'd accomplished the task set down by his father despite Caledon's constant, distracting presence in the shadows. Not that Hadrian was of a mind to protest. Whenever he felt a strong hand closing around his arm to drag him backwards into the concealment of an alley, whenever he turned a corner to find himself face to face with the handsome blond, it was to receive a quick, passionate kiss or a discreet caress that left Hadrian burning. He was as close to rapture as he ever expected to be. He didn't want to return to Shard's Point ever.

The sunlight left him blinking as he exited the latest inn. Immediately a hand took hold of his elbow from behind.

"Keep walking, love."

Hadrian suppressed a smile as realized he was being led back to Caledon's inn. "So soon? That interview was only a few minutes."

"I'm quick to recover. One of my many talents."

Hadrian ducked his head, looking around from beneath

his lashes to be sure no one guessed their intentions. "It's so soon..."

Caledon turned him around. The mercenary's blue eyes were narrowed. "Did I hurt you the last time? Are you sore? I hadn't meant to be so rough—"

The other man's obvious concern filled Hadrian with a yearning he didn't know how to explain. He reached up and caressed a tanned cheek. "No, you didn't hurt me at all. I was only teasing you." Hadrian reddened. "I enjoyed that last time. You were very... determined."

No longer worried, Caledon now looked smug. "You were rather loud that time. I was amazed no one knocked on the door to see what was the matter." He laughed when Hadrian's color deepened. "So will you let me steal you away for a few minutes? I've missed you."

Hadrian looked up from beneath his lashes. "It had better be more than a few minutes," he murmured.

Caledon smirked, reaching up to cup the other man's chin. "Be careful what you wish for, love."

If you only knew, Hadrian thought, looking up at the taller man wistfully. He had never expected lust to feel this way, as though he would die if he didn't see Caledon and yet be nearly sick with anticipation when they were together. Every breath he took was a measurement of time: the stolen moments spent with Caledon that were too painfully short—or the agonizing moments when they were apart and every second lasted a lifetime.

Hadrian was familiar with addiction; he'd been exposed to it during his encounters with his father's worshippers, the Dimorada. This thing he felt for Caledon, it made him think of those drug-addled men and women who would give anything for another taste of their drug. Caledon was his drug. The mercenary left him high and flying. When they were apart his absence left Hadrian pacing the borders of desperation.

To his surprise, Caledon steered him past the inn and led Hadrian away from the city's center.

"I want to take you beneath the sun," the mercenary murmured, a hint of shyness on his normally bold face. Emotion seized Hadrian's heart at the glimpse of vulnerability in the strong man. He wanted to wrap his arms around Caledon and embrace him so tightly that they became one entity. He settled with squeezing the mercenary's hand. Caledon smiled down at him as though he understood.

At the outskirts of town the mercenary guided him to a copse of trees. Hadrian saw an occasional wooden toy discarded within the grass, the ragged end of a rope hanging from a tree. This was a place children made much use of. But thankfully no younglings were about at this hour.

Caledon drew him down beneath the shade of a gnarled oak tree and there began to tenderly make love to him. Hadrian clutched at the grass and sighed. He dug his heels into the soil and arched beneath the other man's gentle caresses. He ran his hands over every inch of Caledon that he could reach and smiled with joy when he heard the older man groan. If this is lust, he thought, delirious, then what must love be like? He didn't think there could be much of a difference. Not when Caledon looked down at him with shining blue eyes and Hadrian imagined he could see the other man's heart there.

Love and lust. To Hadrian they had become one and the same. Even if someone later proved him wrong, for this time it was all he wanted.

Caledon was disappointed with himself. He'd managed to break only one leg of the bed he and Hadrian currently lay sprawled upon. He would have to work on his technique.

Hadrian was a drowsy warmth along his side. Caledon tightened his arm around pale shoulders and drew the younger man closer against him. Hadrian murmured in his sleep, his head pillowed on Caledon's shoulder, one leg draped across the mercenary's thighs. Caledon looked down at him as his free hand took a leisurely sweep down the slender back.

He would miss this, he realized. He would miss Hadrian. Caledon had yet to meet a more compatible lover and that was a considerable feat. Hadrian accepted Caledon's advances without protest. Truly, he received Caledon with a hunger that served to fire the mercenary to new heights. The more Caledon wanted, the more Hadrian gave until they seemed on the verge of combusting from the sheer fury of their lovemaking.

A satisfied smile curved Caledon's lips. Yes, he had well-used the younger man to no complaints, but Hadrian was still as innocent as they came. Caledon had kept his sexual explorations on the tamer side but he could tell with every gasp and moan for more that it was only a matter of time before Hadrian was ready for some experimentation. Hadrian was a banked fire that needed someone to ignite him. Caledon was more than willing to be that source of fuel.

Caledon turned his head on the pillow and looked out the window of his room. The sky was brightening from the pink light of dawn. This was the day he dreaded, the day Hadrian would leave for home. True, it would only be a fortnight before Hadrian returned with his father, but Caledon could already tell that the weeks in between would be torture for him.

"Why do you look so sad?"

Caledon smiled down at the grey gaze that blinked up at him. Hadrian's wide eyes were sleepy and soft. It was one of the mercenary's favorite sights. "You're leaving me today."

"Only for a short while."

"Even a day will be too long."

A weighted pause followed his response. Caledon,

rarely nervous, felt his palms begin to sweat.

Hadrian rested his chin on Caledon's chest, hesitance on his face. "Do you—do you really mean that? Have you enjoyed being with me as much as I've loved being with you?"

The hint of color that touched Hadrian's cheek made Caledon's spine melt. Rarely did the women he sleep with blush anymore. "I mean it, love. I've grown accustomed to your pretty face and to your pretty body and to those pretty sounds you make whenever I lick you down between—"

"Stop that!" Hadrian blurted, red-faced and flustered. He laughed. "You're terrible."

Caledon bent his head and kissed the tip of the younger man's nose. "And you're adorable when you're embarrassed." He tilted Hadrian's chin up. "Now kiss me. It's the surest way to shut me up."

He pressed his mouth against the younger man's, marveling as always at the softness that met his lips, the submissive yield of Hadrian's mouth beneath his own. It had been a long time since the mercenary had been trusted with anything so completely. It made him slide his arms around Hadrian's back and roll the slighter man atop him. He slipped his tongue into Hadrian's mouth and listened to him moan.

When Caledon broke the kiss, Hadrian's head dropped against the mercenary's collarbone, lashes lying thick and still upon his pale cheeks. The full puff of his lips invited the mercenary to taste him again but Caledon resisted. He was seized with an urge to say something, to speak words he had never spoken to another lover, man or woman. He bit his tongue to stop himself. He stroked the sides of Hadrian's face, smiling at the contented expression on the fair features.

"Open your eyes, love."

Hadrian lifted his lashes and Caledon saw how the raven-black discs of his pupils consumed most of the silver irises. It was the look of desire, of lust. Maybe, of more.

"Keep looking at me," Caledon whispered.

He slid his hand down the pale body, over dips and valleys he had mapped with lips and tongue, over landscape he knew had been previously uncharted by anyone. All mine, Caledon thought, watching Hadrian's lips part when Caledon skimmed over the plump curve of his buttock.

Emotion darkened Hadrian's eyes to pewter. "What do you mean?" he said, reaching up to touch a lock of golden hair.

Caledon's heart stuttered. Had he said the words aloud? He hoped he hadn't... And yet perversely, a part of him hoped that he had, and that Hadrian had understood.

"Just keep looking at me," Caledon replied, lifting his head to taste briefly of the lips he couldn't resist. "Let me see you."

He coaxed Hadrian to open his legs, guiding them fall to either side of Caledon. He slid a warm palm up the back of a shapely thigh and he let his other hand slip between their abdomens.

"Sit up, love."

He knew Hadrian was uncomfortable with this position. But Caledon was determined to make him like it if only for this once. Holding back his smile as Hadrian looked everywhere but at him, Caledon urged him up. The pale column of the younger man's sex rose up between them and Caledon gently folded his fingers around it. Hadrian sighed, his eyes closing as Caledon slowly stroked him from base to tip. With his hand on a rounded buttock, he encouraged Hadrian to rock his hips. After a moment, Hadrian no longer needed the guidance as his hands fell to Caledon's chest and his body rolled in rhythm into the mercenary's hand.

Caledon just watched him. He memorized the way arousal stained Hadrian's cheeks before the flush spread down his neck to the top of his chest. He studied the way the pert, pink nipples hardened into rosy stones when he ran a thumb across them and how Hadrian bit his lip when Caledon squeezed the tiny buds. His ears filled with the sounds Hadrian's soft, panting breaths, the occasional moan he gave when Caledon rubbed his palm over the head of his cock. Caled was constructing memories. It saddened him to do it but he knew he had to. Hadrian wouldn't be with him much longer. Only a few, precious hours.

Caledon gathered the copious liquid that now leaked from the head of Hadrian's length and slicked his fingers with it. Stroking the younger man a little faster, Caledon reached behind the pale body and delved between the spread buttocks. Hadrian's eyes flew open when the first finger scraped lightly across his opening. Then his lashes fell to half-mast as Caledon circled and teased the puckered flesh, rubbing promisingly across it but never breaching it.

"Please, Caledon."

The whispered entreaty, something Hadrian would have been too shy to do just days before, made Caledon's cock harden.

"Please what?" he teased.

Stubbornness flashed in the grey eyes. Caledon just smirked. "You know I'm going to make you say it, so don't fight me." He squeezed Hadrian's erection, earning a throaty groan. The sound made the mercenary shift restlessly beneath him. "The longer you fight me, the longer it'll take you to get what you want. So just... say it."

Caledon rubbed his finger a little harder across Hadrian's opening. The tip of his finger tickled the edges, not quite sliding inside. Hadrian whimpered and clutched at Caledon's shoulders with his nails. He rolled his hips, trying to push the digit inside, but Caledon chuckled and moved his fingers back to circling the pink flesh. "Say it, love."

"You're so cruel," Hadrian panted but there was a smile

on his lips. He moaned and pushed himself down against Caledon's stiff cock. "Please, Caledon," he murmured, grey eyes swirling like a building storm as he looked down at the mercenary, "please... take me."

Caledon groaned and pushed two fingers into Hadrian's body. Hadrian's mouth fell open, his eyes shutting completely.

"Caledon!"

The mercenary forgot his teasing and plunged his fingers deeper into the slender body above him. Hadrian shuddered and groaned, his thighs closing around Caledon's hips as he lifted himself up and down on the fingers that impaled him. Caledon licked his lips and stroked Hadrian's length with more urgency, his own passion rising with every sign that Hadrian's was peaking.

He was painfully hard from simply watching Hadrian. He wanted to slide his fingers out and slam himself home. But he waited, teasing, tormenting. His fingers found that spot inside the younger man that made him shudder.

"Nnnh, yes!"

Caledon bit the inside of his cheek, struggling not to find his own release as Hadrian writhed on his fingers.

"Show me how you want to ride me," Caledon said in a thickened voice. "Give me a taste, love."

Hadrian emitted a choked sound and rocked his hips onto Caledon's hand. Caledon pumped his fingers faster into Hadrian's tight channel, groaning a little as he felt the muscles constricting around his fingers. He rubbed hard over Hadrian's pleasure spot, pressing down on it as he simultaneously squeezed the younger man's weeping shaft.

Hadrian cried out, stiffening in Caledon's lap. Hot liquid streaked up Hadrian's stomach and dripped down onto the mercenary's chest. Caledon grabbed Hadrian by the hips and swiftly rolled them over. Hadrian looked up from the depths of the pillows, panting, his eyes heavy lidded. Caledon wanted to hide him away, to stow him someplace secret where no one would ever find him. Only

Caledon's. Only his.

A rough sound caught in Caledon's throat as he lifted pale legs to his shoulders and flexed his hips forward. Hadrian bit off a cry and clutched at the mercenary's forearms. Caledon looked down at the beautiful face as it contorted into an expression of pain and pleasure. He drove himself in all the way to the hilt and felt as though he'd come finally home.

Hadrian made short work of him after that. The sight of the younger man's pale throat arched back as the dark head thrashed upon the pillows was too much for Caledon. He gripped Hadrian's legs and thrust hard and quick, short, fierce jabs that had Hadrian gasping, his grey eyes rolling up into his head.

"Gods, love," Caledon gasped. "You're so beautiful. So beautiful..."

And then it was too much. Caledon felt his release surge through him from the tips of his toes to the top of his head. He groaned and shoved himself as deep into Hadrian's body as he could before spilling himself into the welcoming heat. A clipped off cry from beneath him told him that he hadn't found his pleasure alone.

Hadrian pulled him down and covered his face with sloppy kisses. Caledon laughed and tried to return the same. Their lips ended up bruised, but it didn't matter.

"Caledon," Hadrian breathed against his mouth. "Oh, Caledon, I don't want to leave."

The mercenary pressed his cheek against the other man's and hugged him fiercely. "After you return here with your father, I'm going back with you."

The minute the words left his lips, he questioned his sanity. He'd not committed himself to anyone ever. What was the use, when there were so many willing to share his bed without promises for more? But the prospect of doing this with someone else no longer seemed appealing to Caledon. Tired, well-used bodies with too much experience... he decided at that moment that he was through with that. He wanted to be clean again. He wanted lovemaking to be special. He laughed inwardly. What a woman he'd become! But the truth of the matter was that he wanted his innocence again.

"I'm going back with you," he repeated firmly.

When Caledon raised his head and looked into Hadrian's eyes he saw that the dark-haired beauty knew exactly what he meant.

"You're coming back with me," Hadrian whispered. "I'm afraid to believe it."

Caledon smiled gently. "Believe it."

Hadrian was hurt. He didn't understand.

"I can't see you off," Caledon told him. "It's just something I can't do."

The mercenary sighed as Hadrian continued to look down at him with dark eyes. "Gods, Hadrian, you look as though I kicked your dog." Caledon ran a hand through his hair in agitation. "Just go, will you? I'll see you again in a fortnight. It won't be long. I refuse to say farewell for so inconsequential a time."

Brave words when he didn't believe them himself.

"Then you're not mad at me?"

Caledon groaned and reached up to Hadrian's tunic. He grabbed a fistful of fabric and pulled the younger man down to him. He kissed Hadrian slow and deep, using his tongue the way he knew made the younger man melt. When he pulled back, Hadrian looked on the verge of falling out of his saddle. Caledon laughed affectionately and pushed him back upright. "Still think I'm mad at you?"

Hadrian touched his lips. He smiled then, relieved and blissful in a way that Caledon knew was entirely because of him. It made the mercenary's chest swell. "Be waiting for me," Hadrian told him, gathering up the reins. He lightly touched Caledon's hair before reaching into a bag at his waist. He pulled out something and pressed it shyly into the mercenary's hand. "Until you see me again."

Caledon closed his fist and stepped back as Hadrian spurred his horse. Caledon didn't wait to watch him leave; he turned and began walking resolutely back towards the Bell &Buckle. It wasn't until the sound of hoof beats faded that Caledon opened his hand. In his palm lay a blue ribbon, twined around a lock of silky black hair.

Weakness for shadow. Someday, Caledon mused, it will be my downfall.

Hadrian had been gone all of eight days. Caledon wouldn't last the rest.

He was a mess and he knew it. He didn't bother to raise his head from the pillow of his forearms as a body jarred his table. If someone wanted a fight, he was in no condition to offer one.

"Gods, Caledon, will you look at yourself? I'm sorry to say it, but I'm a bit ashamed to admit to knowing you."

Caledon sighed against the sticky wood and lifted his head. He blinked groggily at Tye, who was seated across from him and looking thoroughly disgusted. "Then don't admit it," he said in a hoarse voice.

Tye shook his head and tucked dirty brown hair behind on ear. "Well, seeing as I'm your best friend, I don't feel comfortable doing that." The lanky mercenary sat back in his chair and regarded his friend pityingly. "You look awful. Can you clean yourself up some? You're a damned sight."

Caledon shrugged. He didn't care what he looked like. He wasn't out to catch anyone's eye now that Hadrian had left.

"What if your boy comes back early, eh? Perhaps thinking to surprise you? He catches sight—and wind, might I add—of you like this and you'd better believe he'll think twice about sharing that pretty body with you."

"Shut up," Caledon grumbled, heaving himself back into his chair with a grunt. "He'd still want me. He's in love with me."

Tye raised an eyebrow. "He said that to you?"

Caledon smiled slightly. "Not exactly. But I've seen it often enough. I know the look."

"And yet this doesn't bother you," Tye said slowly, thoughtfully.

Caledon didn't even think. "Of course not."

Tye smirked then, the sight of which made Caledon's spine stiffen. "Funny, seems to me I recall that you hated it whenever a pretty lass declared that she'd lost her heart to you. You always said that love was something you didn't want from your bedmates. Love, as I recall you telling me once, was an emotion that had no business bouncing around in your bed."

A hundred glib responses found their way to Caledon's tongue. In the end he decided to discard them all. He leaned forward and pinned his friend with a frank look. "I was wrong."

Brown eyes rounded. "By the gods. Y-you're in love with him?"

Caledon rubbed a hand over his stubbled jaw. He really did need to shave. "All I know is that it's killing me not to be near him right now. And when I think of the future—" Caledon felt his cheeks warm, " —he's in it."

"So you really are besotted," Tye mused. He suddenly threw back his head and let loose a loud guffaw that turned several head within the tavern. "And for a pretty boy, no less. Ah, gods, Caledon, and here I thought I knew you."

Caledon glared at him. "I'm thrilled to have surprised you."

"Damn. I wish I hadn't taken that job for Hanamon. I admit I thought your pretty friend was attractive when he met me for business, but if I'd known he'd become so important to you I would have remained."

Caledon also regretted that his best friend had left town so soon after Hadrian arrived. Given the opportunity, Hadrian and Tye would have gotten along well, he was sure of it. "No matter," he said with a careless shrug. "You'll see him again when he returns with his father. You're accepting the position, yes?"

"Ah, I don't know. I'd planned on returning home to my mother and sister." Tye winked a brown eye. "After this job for Hanamon, I've got some extra coin I'd like to give them."

"Just wait awhile," Caledon insisted. "It would mean a lot to me if you got to know him." His eyes fell away. "Maybe you'll be able to see him with clearer eyes than mine. You might be able to tell if I'm being a fool in this."

"Caledon."

He raised his eyes at the warm voice.

Tye smiled genuinely at him, no humor or mockery in it. "I've never heard you speak this way about anyone else, nor have I see you moon so. I truly doubt that what you're feeling is false. You're too experienced in these things to fall blindly."

"Perhaps you're right, but I'd like to be certain all the same. Tell me you'll stay. You don't have to accept the job with his father. I just want you to see him. "

"Alright, my friend. I'll delay my trip another week."

Caledon relaxed with a smile. This was the only thing that had picked up his spirits of late. "You won't regret this. You're going to love him," he assured the lanky mercenary.

"I hope not!" Tye said with a laugh. "I'm leaving that up to you, old man."

Caledon grinned cockily. "As long as you know your place."

Tye just groaned.

"You can't postpone your trip? They'll be here in two days," Caledon protested.

His thief friends, Gam and Lio, were perched atop a splintered, grey fence, tossing a coin back and forth between them. Caledon watched Lio deftly flick the coin between his fingers before tossing it across to the other man. The thieves did this two more times before Caledon reached out and snatched the coin from the air. "Are you listening to me?"

Gam rolled his hazel eye. "Your cock is besotted with that pretty thing you tossed in the loft. Yes, we understand. But our apologies, Caledon, the prospect of meeting him isn't so grand an event that it could deter us from a rather lucrative business transaction."

Caledon smirked at that. "What is it this time? Another blind trader with a cart full of precious Kenwyn glass?"

Lio frowned, affronted. "So that information was slightly off."

"He wasn't blind and he wasn't carrying Kenwyn glass."

"So?" Lio retorted, narrowing his single green eye at the mercenary. "At least we managed to salvage the hit."

"By sleeping with the trader's daughter," Caledon scoffed. "And didn't you tell me she gave you some sort of rash—"

"Oh, go away!" Lio snapped, crossing his arms in a huff.

Gam chuckled. "Look, Caledon, we'd love to meet your new interest. Really we would. I mean, the sounds he was making that night were enough to stir one's imagination—"

"Gam," the mercenary warned.

The thief attempted to look contrite. "The timing is bad, that's all. The tip we got says cinnamon is being carted to Hanta. Cinnamon! Do you know how much we could sell that for in the flatlands?" When Caledon remained unmoved, Gam hopped down from the fence and slung an arm around the taller man's shoulders. "Look, if you're all that bent on him I'm sure we'll see him again, right? After all, you intend to be with him for the conceivable future, true?"

"Yes," Caledon replied grudgingly. He gave a disappointed sigh. "Alright. Next time. I'm traveling with him to his home so I won't see you for awhile, but I'm keeping you to your word when we come back."

Lio looked irritated still, but crossed his heart with his fingers. "If you're still with him, we'll meet him. Though what could be so infatuating about him is beyond me."

Caledon grinned. "Just you wait and see, Lio. I guarantee that even you will fall for him."

Lio scowled. "I doubt it."

"Just wait."

The longest fortnight in Juxtan's history had finally passed. It was nothing less than a miracle. Caledon couldn't eat breakfast and was afraid to drink for fear he'd end up sloshed just as Hadrian and his father arrived. He was a wreck and he hated it. He was as nervous as he'd been on his first job so many years ago as he now roamed the streets of Rhiad, eyes alert for new faces that entered the streets.

"Caledon, catch!"

He speared the thrown apple on his dagger and grinned. "Well, many thanks, Mistress Alena." He sauntered over to the redhead and leaned on her fruit cart. "And how are you this lovely day?"

The girl blushed, brightening her many freckles. "Not as well as you are, Caledon. The serving girls at the B&B have started a rumor about you, you know."

Caledon grinned. "Oh, and what does it say?"

She glanced up shyly. "That you're in love."

Gods, had he been that obvious? Caledon gave a slightly embarrassed laugh. "Yes, well, don't believe everything you hear, Mistress Alena." He winked. "Then again, maybe you should."

"Ooh, then it's true!" the girl said, clapping her hands happily. "Who is it? You must tell me! I promise I won't tell a soul. Is it Anna? Or what about Junea? I see you looking at her all the time."

Both were pretty barmaids that Caledon had bedded often enough. Neither, however, had been able to keep his interest for very long. "Sorry, love. I can't say."

Alena pouted. "That's so unfair. You're deliberately teasing me."

Caledon took a bite of the crisp apple, chewing thoughtfully. "Let me make it up to you. What's your man doing for work these days?"

"Fyen's been mending fences for Master Lewyn. Sometimes he manages to pick up a job here and there at the docks. Why?"

"Tell Fyen to come to the Mercenary's Guild tonight. If he's interested, my friend has a job for him that will pay better than anything he's done of late."

Alena's green eyes widened. "Oh, do you think so? Fyen could really use something with decent pay. Master Lewyn misuses him something awful."

Satisfaction made Caledon feel ten feet tall. "I promise you, love: tell your man to come to the Guild and you'll both be happy that he did."

A wet kiss found its way to his cheek.

"You're such a sweetie, Caledon."

"You're welcome, love." Caledon winked. "I'm happy to do it."

It was probably the stupidest idea he had ever come up with. Ridiculous, even. How could he be harboring any feelings other than lust for Hadrian? By the gods, Caledon barely knew him. And what he did know about the younger man tended more towards what pleasured Hadrian physically more than anything else.

"You've been acting like a fool," Caledon muttered to himself as he tugged on the freshly washed hem of his tunic. He patted his hair, hoping it wasn't awfully unruly. For the first time in his life he'd spent coin on a hair tonic. His face still burned at the memory. "Hadrian was a delightful tumble. Nothing more. Don't overreact. You're not ruled by your cock, are you?"

Of course not. Caledon ni Agthon was his own man. He did what he wanted and to whom he wanted and no one returned the favor. No one could say that they'd ever bent Caledon to their whims. No one could claim to have held anything other than his brief, sexual interest. He didn't parcel himself out that way. Oh, no. Caledon ni Agthon was not easy.

Oh, but he felt easy. Caledon closed his eyes and let his head roll forward on his neck, trying to ease the ache of tension that had been steadily mounting as the day progressed. Hadrian and his father were in town at this very moment and Caledon felt like heaving up the contents of his stomach.

Horrible, emasculating thoughts assailed him. What if Hadrian was no longer interested in him? What if the younger man returned and after seeing him, Caledon realized he no longer felt that spark of attraction? What if Caledon had spent this past fortnight creating a relationship that didn't exist except in his mind?

Caledon groaned aloud. "My biggest fear has come true." He slapped his forehead. "I've turned into a woman."

Disgusted with himself, Caledon self-consciously straightened his belt and continued walking down the street. He noticed the unusual number of horses tied up outside the large building that housed the Mercenary's Guild. Excitement and trepidation made his pulse run.

A gust of wind ruffled his hair. Cursing, he tried to pat

down the somewhat stiff golden spikes. Blasted merchant, he thought in irritation. He'd said this wouldn't make my hair harden up! He suddenly realized what he'd been thinking and groaned again. Gods, he was worried about his hair of all things! Defiantly, Caledon raked his fingers through the stiff mass atop his head. Who cares what his hair looked like? He was a man. A mercenary. He was expected to look a little rough. But as he paused at the doors of the Guild, he couldn't help patting down a few wayward strands.

Pathetic.

He pulled at the heavy doors. They didn't budge. He took a deep breath and tried again, pulling at the scarred iron handles. They shifted slightly, then stopped as though locked from inside.

Gods, was he that late for the meeting?

"You idiot," he cursed himself, jogging around the building. He hadn't wanted to be obvious, had wanted to salvage some dignity by not being the first to show up even though he'd wanted to be there hours ago, waiting breathlessly for Hadrian to return. Caledon had his pride. He wanted to keep some of it. Maybe he shouldn't have worried so much about that.

The Guild was a large building and he crossed some distance before he came to the side door that was rarely used. He pushed experimentally on the door and sighed in relief when it easily swung inwards.

Pausing on the threshold, he decided to quit fooling himself. Now that the initial fear of being locked out of the meeting had faded, Caledon could no longer pretend that he wasn't anxious to see the younger man. He needed to see Hadrian like he needed to see the sun every morning. Smiling somewhat stupidly, he slipped inside the building.

He was in one of the halls that led to the Guild's backrooms. It was here in these hidden rooms that the guild masters did their unsavory business. It was dark, but he could see the light of the main room ahead. The sounds of many raised voices quickened his step. So close.

But to his frustration and dismay, his way was blocked by a wall of men spilling out from the main room into the hall. For them to have needed to stand this far back meant that well over a hundred mercenaries must be filling the room. Caledon grinned in approval. Hadrian had done his job well.

Perhaps too well. His smile faded when he realized he was unable to push into the room. Mercenaries were not a type to yield kindly. Caledon didn't even bother trying to push his way through. He wasn't in the mood for a fight. He moved along the line of men until he found a thin gap between which he could see the front of the room where a dais stretched along its length.

There were three men standing on the rise. Caledon's lips curled into a sneer when he recognized one of the handful of greedy, unscrupulous guild masters. The fat man—why were they always fat?—was rubbing his hands with obvious avarice, eager for his cut for bringing so many mercenaries here. Caledon's eyes skittered away from that unpleasant sight, moving onto a tall, imposing figure in white robes that stood beside him. He took in the man's midnight black hair streaked with distinctive strands of silver and the cleanly cut black beard that framed a strong, stubborn jaw. Even before Caledon saw the man's eyes—crystalline silver—he knew who this man was.

He wanted to feel a rush of kinship with the man. Here was Hadrian's father, the man who had raised him. And yet when Caledon looked into the hard, imposing expression on the man's face he felt a chill of unease pass over his skin. This was the man who had left Hadrian unused to touch. This was the man whose love was so insubstantial that Hadrian didn't recognize the emotion even though Caledon had seen it clearly in the other man's eyes. Caledon wanted to like him, for Hadrian's sake. But studying the cold, somewhat arrogant lines of the man's face, Caledon realized it was going to take a considerable effort to warm up to the man.

Unhappy with this realization, he let his eyes fall to the man's left. It was like stepping from a snowstorm to be enveloped by a thick, warm blanket. Caledon smiled, uncaring that he looked like a lovesick fool. He'd harbored a small but substantial fear that his remembrance of Hadrian had been false. It was not. Hadrian was still as beautiful and pale as an ice sculpture glittering in the sun of the mercenary's memories. Caledon's heart swelled. Now that he'd seen Hadrian again he couldn't deny the truth: Caledon was in love with him.

Caledon stood taller with pride as he gazed at the object of his heart's affections. He knew without looking that most eyes in the room were on Hadrian. He didn't blame his fellow mercenaries. Hadrian was a gem in Rhiad, utterly priceless. But he was Caledon's gem and the mercenary looked forward to the time spent after the meeting when he could remind the younger man of that very fact.

Caledon strained to the tips of his boots, trying to make himself visible above the crowd. He waved his hand, trying to catch Hadrian's attention. But Hadrian was looking at the floor of the dais, his grey eyes blank. His expression, like a wall of ice, bothered Caledon somewhat, but he chalked it up to nervousness. Perhaps he was unused to being in front of so large a crowd. Caledon glanced at Hadrian's father again. Or perhaps there were other reasons. The man was unquestioningly intimidating as he spoke, his smooth, cultured voice seeping over them all like a heavy pall.

"I thank you all for taking the time to be here," Hadrian's father said. "I am Gavedon ni Leyanon. It is by my invitation that you are here."

A small murmur began at the far end of the room. Caledon was unsure of the disturbance. He was trying not be perturbed by the fact that Gavedon hadn't bothered to introduce his son.

Gavedon smiled. He was a handsome man, Caledon would give him that. Hadrian would probably age to look much like him, though with the softer touches to his face that Caledon now realized must have come from Hadrian's mother. But though Gavedon was attractive, his looks held a curious emptiness. To Caledon he was like a cold glass window that looked upon a shadowed room.

"I see that some of you recognize my name," Gavedon continued, still smiling.

Uncomfortable with the man's smile, Caledon spared a look at the crowd of mercenaries. He saw young Fyen, Alena's man, at the side of the room looking eager and excited at the prospect of well-paying work. Caledon smiled to see him. Towards the front, near the dais, Caledon spied Tye. There was a frown of mistrust on Tye's face.

Troubled by his friend's expression, Caledon returned his attention to the dais. Hadrian remained staring at the floor, for all the world looking as though he were in a trance. Unease built within Caledon. Years spent listening to his instincts had him double-checking his route down the hallway to see that it was clear. He mentally shook himself. There was nothing to fear here. He was in a room full of heavily-armed, well-trained men.

"For those who do not know me," Gavedon continued, "let me introduce myself. I am the Gavedon ni Leyanon, who founded the Order of the White Shard. It is by the Order's business that you are here. I have no need for an army of mercenaries. I have no need of any of you at all."

Sorcery!

The word rolled through the crowd like a tumbleweed. Caledon's eyes shot to Hadrian. A sick feeling was beginning to burn in his stomach.

"What are you, a mage in disguise? Or worse, a sorcerer?"

"Would that be so bad?"

Caledon shook his head. He closed his ears to the

increasingly agitated murmurs from the crowd. They were mistaken... A sudden shout from the back of the room made all eyes turn around.

"The doors are locked! What treachery is this?!"

"No," Caledon whispered. He knew at once that more was amiss here than he comprehended.

"Thank you again for coming, gentlemen," Gavedon said, his voice remaining smooth and controlled despite the rising shouts and the pounding against the doors. "You've made my task a much easier one."

Through the shouting and jostling as men began to push for the door Caledon heard Gavedon speak to Hadrian. "It is time," he said to his son. For the first time since his father had begun speaking, Hadrian raised his face. His eyes were as hard and dull as stone as they looked out upon the throng. He spoke a single word: "*Fire*," and the nightmare began.

Caledon had never seen sorcery at work. He didn't know that fire could be conjured from the air, that it could roll out like a twitching, golden rug and swamp a line of men in its path. Screams filled the air; smoke began to rise up to the high ceilings. Caledon stared aghast as he saw men burst into flame, clothes and hair streaming with fire. A mad rush began for the doors. Men were trampled in the frenzy. Some were crushed against the walls. The stench of burning meat and hair began to thicken the air and when Caledon caught whiff of it he bent and gagged.

More flame filled the room, flaring to reach from wall to wall. Caledon retreated back into the dark hallway, avoiding the stampeding mercenaries as they sought the main doors. The air above the crowd shimmered with heat and smoke. Choking and retching on the smells, Caledon peered through the undulating air to the dais.

In spite of all that was occurring before his very eyes, Caledon refused to believe what was happening. This was a mistake. A dream. Hadrian was an innocent, the most harmless creature Caledon had ever come across. Surely this was some trick of his imagination. It had to be.

But he found Hadrian and his father still in place. And although Hadrian's beautiful face was untouched by the stress and trauma of what was happening before him, Caledon could read his lips forming the same word over and over: *fire*.

Caledon wanted to scream his denial. Hadrian couldn't be a sorcerer. It was impossible. Yet his memory held those bits of conversation whose meaning Caledon hadn't looked deeper into. He remembered all of those claims Hadrian had made about how capable he was of taking care of himself despite lacking skill with a weapon. Had he thought Hadrian was bluffing? Hadrian, as had become perfectly, painfully clear, had been telling the truth.

Rage filled Caledon. Betrayal. He looked with wild eyes at his fellows—friends he had spent most of his life with—as they howled and screamed as they were consumed by sorcerous fire. His hand went to a dagger and he hefted it, wanting to hurl it with all his might at the men on the dais. But before he could cock his arm back for the throw, a wall of flame swept towards him. He dove into the hallway and felt the heat sear his back, singeing his hair. He gasped against the floor, finding the air too thin and smoky to fill his lungs. Choking, he climbed to his feet and staggered down the hallway.

He burst through the door and coughed in the crisp evening air. From the front of the Guild he heard the doors bang open as the mercenaries finally smashed through it. Greasy black smoke spilled out into the street, trailing like greedy fingers after the men who ran from the building. Some were bloodied from the trampling inside. Some—oh, gods—were hideously burned or on fire, collapsing to the dirt to roll in it.

Caledon limped towards them, looking for Tye. Just as he reached the front of the building a ball of fire burst from the front doors. Screams rent the air as the mercantile across the street from the Guild exploded into flame. Shopkeepers and customers ran out only to be drenched in scalding fire as it burst from the Guild again.

"Gods!" Caledon cried, his voice cracked. These were people he knew, people he spoke with every day and they were burning. "Over here!" he shouted at a young woman who'd lost her sense of direction in her panic. "Over here!"

She turned to him, a brief relief clearing her horrified face. She started towards him when a tongue of flame licked out and wrapped itself around her. Caledon's screamed echoed the woman's as she pinwheeled away, batting at the flames that blackened her skin.

Caledon sobbed and tore at his hair. He needed to find Tye. He needed to get his friend out of here...

"Fire!"

Caledon spun on his heels, nearly tripping in his fear. Gavedon and Hadrian had exited through the front doors of the burning Guild. Behind them, the roof of the building crashed down in an explosion of wood and flame. Caledon staggered backwards, throwing himself around the corner of a tavern. He watched the two dark-haired men split up, heading in opposite directions down the street. Hadrian was heading his way.

Caledon lost his mind then. Rage flooded his veins, making him shake so hard his limbs threatened to tear off.

"Hadrian!" he screamed, storming out into the street. "What are you doing?!"

Fire answered him, billowing across the street like golden banners.

Caledon sobbed, wiping at his soot stained face as tears of anger and grief threatened to blind him. "You bastard!" he cried out, his voice cracking. "Why are you doing this? *Tell me why?*"

The black-haired sorcerer continued to advance, following the trumpeting of more sorcerous flame and the horrific chorus of human suffering.

Caledon choked on his own tears. Strength left him and he fell to his knees. Hadrian's blank gaze fell on Caledon then passed over him as though he didn't exist.

"*Fire,*" he said again.

Caledon fell onto his back as a cloud of flame roared over him. He covered his face with his arms as fiery heat threatened to burn off his skin. Above him, he heard more agonized screaming. Wood cracked and snapped as more buildings caught fire. A deafening roar shook the ground as the mercantile collapsed into a heap of flaming wreckage.

Caledon rolled over and coughed into the dust. When he managed to raise his head, Hadrian had turned away from him and was sending fire after a group of fleeing mercenaries. Caledon knew those men. He'd played cards with them only yesterday. Run, he thought desperately. *Please get away.*

But fire knocked them down like wooden toys. Their bodies burned just as easily.

Caledon wept into the dirt. This was his fault. He had brought these men here, he had encouraged them—gods, he had overcome their reservations and pressured them to be here. He knew in his heart that Fyen must be dead. Ah, gods, Alena, forgive me... And his best friend—

His thoughts seemed to magickally summon Tye. Caledon looked up with wide eyes as he heard a familiar voice scream from down the street.

"You won't get away with this, you murderer!"

Caledon looked on in rising horror. "Tye, don't!"

But his best friend, mad with grief, didn't hear him. Tye rushed at Hadrian's back with his sword drawn, tears streaked down his smoke-smudged face. When Caledon felt a spark of fear for Hadrian, the mercenary ground his teeth in self-hatred. *No mercy! No mercy for him!*

But any fear for the sorcerer was wasted. Caledon should have known better, he realized bitterly. Tye didn't get within ten feet of Hadrian before the sorcerer calmly turned and blasted the mercenary full on with a fist of fire.

Tye's mellow brown eyes burned black. His mouth

opened in a scream that was swallowed by the roaring flame around him. His head was a cap of fire. His limbs were flailing ribbons of gold. He spun once before collapsing to the dirt where his body twitched and smoldered.

It was the last thing Caledon saw before he went mad. Shrieking Tye's name, he lurched to his feet and sprinted towards the smoking lump in the street. He didn't care that Hadrian turned towards him. He didn't care that the soulless silver gaze was pinned upon him. Let me die. Burn me. Flame rushed past Caledon so close that his clothes smoked. The force of the shooting fire lifted him off his feet. He crashed into some discarded kegs beside the ruins of what had once been a notary and he lay there, moaning in pain.

Consciousness flickered teasingly. He heard sounds he never wanted to hear again—the screams of those being burned alive, the wails of those watching their loved ones die. The air was so thick with the stench of fire and death that he thought it would never leave his lungs; he would breathe the horrible miasma forever.

Time passed for Caledon without his knowledge.

Gradually, his wits cleared. He blinked painfully, slowly realizing where he lay. Like an old man he crawled on hands and knees out of the refuse towards the street. He saw no sign of either Hadrian or his father. What buildings that had stood here on this street had been reduced to smoking heaps of charcoal. For the first time since Rhiad's founding, Caledon could see all the way to the docks. Not a building still stood to impede his view.

And what a view it was. Black and grey smoke hung like storm clouds over what remained of the city. Some parts of the sky were lit gold and yellow by fires that yet blazed on the ground. Sparks flew up periodically as fire-weakened buildings collapsed to the ground.

Caledon became aware of the weeping, a soft wail like the haunting cry of a thousand mourning spirits. So, there were some who had been left alive. It was a small mercy after what Caledon had seen this night.

He stood on shaky limbs, unafraid that Hadrian or his father would see him and come finish him off. Caledon no longer feared death. He no longer feared a lot of things. A part of him that had once held space for feelings of love and hope was now empty, seared clean by the sorcerous fires that had razed his city. Into that cavernous space he poured his anger, his despair and his fury. He stirred that pot of hatred until it churned. He fanned its flames as surely as the sorcerers had fanned the flames of their destruction.

Caledon turned his eyes to the burned out sky above him and he made a vow. He would find Hadrian and his father. He would hunt them down though it cost him his life and the lives of those around him. He would carve out Gavedon's heart and he would feed it to the man. And when he found Hadrian...

Caledon bent at the waist, his body wracked with heaves. When he found Hadrian he would exact a revenge upon him that befitted the lives of those who were lost here. Killing his father would only be the first step. The first, of many bitter ones.

"I will not sully the name of ni Agthon with what I do now in my course for revenge," he said in a hoarse, smoke-ravaged voice. He coughed and spit up dark phlegm. "From this day forth, I will answer to Caled." His voice rose in volume. "I will be the bane of Gavedon ni Leyanon and his offspring!" His voice cracked, the tissues of his throat tearing. "I will hunt them to the ends of the land!" he continued in an hysterical shout. "Do you hear me? *I will make them pay!*"

Weeping, Caled dropped to his knees. His nails dug bloody furrows in his palm. "I will make them pay," he whispered brokenly, staring at his burning city. "They will pay."

A lock of black hair, bound by a ribbon, fell from his

tunic and lay upon the ground, burned and smoking. Caled stared at it with empty eyes. With a hand that trembled, he pulled his dagger free and stabbed it into the symbol of his love.

PART TWO

CHAPTER FIVE

Gavedon ni Leyanon watched another member of the Order collapse in a storm of flames to join those who had fallen before him. Cries of outrage and horror echoed around the sorcerer's ears but he paid his followers little mind. His eyes were for the man who stood at the edges of the trees, facing off against them as if he thought he could defeat them all.

"Hadrian," he called out, watching the pale face turn in his direction. Gavedon noted dispassionately that Hadrian looked awful: soot and tears streaked his cheeks and his clothing was ripped and smoking from the battle with his latest combatant. "You cannot win this, Hadrian. You cannot defeat them all."

"I don't want to defeat them!" Hadrian cried. He swung his arm wildly to encompass the men and women of the Order of the White Shard who had left the castle to gather behind Gavedon. "This has nothing to do with any of them. My issue is with you!"

Flames lashed out, seeking Gavedon's flesh and illuminating the horrified faces of his followers. Gavedon calmly snuffed the fire out with magecraft.

"We cannot take back what we did at Rhiad. We must move on, Hadrian. We can do nothing else."

"I can do something!" Hadrian retorted, his voice breaking. He dashed the back of a hand across his eyes. "I can stop you so you never do such a thing again. Murderer!"

"And so are you, dear son," Gavedon reminded him. "Your hands are as bloody as mine."

Hadrian nearly crumpled, his grief visible in every line of his body. "I know," he sobbed. "Gods, I know..."

Gavedon saw the white robed figure move into his line of vision. It was the youngest member of the Order, one who was particularly passionate in her worship of Gavedon.

"Die, you traitorous bastard!"

The young woman raised a hand, calling magick. The energy hurtled towards Hadrian like a thrown ball of light. Hadrian staggered back, weary from having previously faced off against nine other sorcerers. But the energy he pulled up to ward off the attack left Gavedon breathless. The old man was right, Gavedon thought, watching his son with perverse pride as Hadrian sent yet another member of the Order to an early grave. Hadrian is as powerful as foreseen.

Lightning cracked across the sky, bringing memories with it...

September 1st, the past…

Gavedon walked through the halls of the castle, his eyes falling disinterestedly upon the flowers strewn across the stones and bundled up and placed against doors. His strong, powerful stride took him through the quiet halls quickly but not quickly enough for him to avoid the white robed men and women who occasionally accosted him, wishing him well.

"A fine night for a babe," wished a young man, a new member to the Order of the White Shard. Once a farmer's son, he had traveled two months to come to Shard's Point

Isle in the hopes that Gavedon would teach him. Fortunately for the young man he possessed the natural ability to magick, otherwise Gavedon would have coldly told him his trip had been wasted. Gavedon did not extend charity.

"We'll see," Gavedon replied curtly but he was unable to help the pride welling up in him. His first child was due to be born this night. His anticipation for the event was high.

He fielded more congratulations as he made his way to his destination: the farthest east tower. Here, enough flowers had been set before a slim wooden door that Gavedon had to literally kick them away to enter the room.

At the sound of his door shutting firmly, the room's sole occupant raised startled eyes.

"My lord, Gavedon!" The old man, far older than the castle's keeper, quickly stood from where he had been studying a book atop a table in the corner of the room. "I expected you to be with your wife at this hour."

"Roisin does not need my presence in order to bear this child," Gavedon replied. In truth, he did not think his wife required him for much at all, anymore. "There is a more urgent matter to which I'd give my attention."

A touch of unease lit the old man's face as he watched Gavedon's eyes drift to the beaten silver bowl that sat upon the table. "My lord?"

"Tell me if this child will be a son," Gavedon said.

The man paled. "But—but in a few more hours—"

"I do not care to wait."

"But, but my lord, you know as well as I that the Council has expressly forbidden the art of scrying within Juxtan." The old man rubbed his hands together anxiously. "We were fortunate that none of the Elders noticed the magickal aura from your first scrying years ago. But to do it again is to invite their notice. And the Council will notice, my lord."

"I do not care," Gavedon said, striding over to the table

and picking up a pitcher of water.

"If we are detected the punishment for scrying is death!" the old man whispered.

Empty silver eyes as icy as the peak upon which Gavedon had learned his power over Life, stabbed into the old man like shards. "I would know the sex of this child and its fate. Suffice it to say I have concerns about my wife's loyalty to me. Better I should know now than after I am stabbed in the back." Those cold eyes narrowed suspiciously. "You would not want to see me fall, would you?"

"Of-of course not!" the old man stammered fearfully. "As the Dimorada claim, you are The One. Without your teachings we are powerless. Ignorant."

Gavedon snorted, content. "Then do this reading for me, old man. I grow impatient and the hour late. From her screeching, my wife will have her babe within the hour."

Shivering at the man's lack of feelings for his wife, the old man waited nervously as Gavedon filled the silver bowl with water.

"Now tell me what you foresee for this child," Gavedon commanded, crossing his arms.

The old man stared into the clear water. As Gavedon waited, the old man nodded.

"The child is a male," he said slowly.

Gavedon's fists clenched. His firstborn was a son. A son. He had to rein in his excitement.

"Tell me, old man, will he inherit my power?"

The old seer frowned, rubbing at his brow as he continued to stare into the bowl. "He will be powerful—very powerful. So strong!" he gasped suddenly. "By the gods..."

Gavedon's lips twitched in pleasure. "You see him as my heir, do you not? He will continue my teachings with the Order."

The old man looked pained. "You know that the readings are rarely so clear," he protested. "With the child not yet born I cannot see his life light beyond mere suggestions of what path he will take. I do see—" the old man broke off, his eyes widening. "Must be wrong," he muttered, shaking his head. "This is unclear, it cannot be correct—"

"What do you see?" Gavedon demanded, staring down into the bowl as if he could glimpse what was disturbing the seer.

"I see a great surge of power. So much energy flowing—the land has never seen its like. And, by the gods, Life drowns out both of your lights, I don't understand"

Gavedon grabbed the man's thin shoulders and shook him violently. "Does my son become my heir?" he demanded. "I don't care about the rest. Tell me if he is my ally or my enemy!"

Shocked, the man stared at Gavedon before slowly nodding and studying the water again. After a long moment in which the howling of the relentless winds outside whistled through the cracks in the castle, the old man let out a soft sigh of pain. "I see what looks to be a great battle. His power is blinding, it is unfathomable." The old man raised his eyes and stepped back. "I see your life light disappear at that moment, but I cannot say for certain that he is the cause."

Gavedon turned away, his shoulders stiff. "My firstborn son will take my life, that is what you are saying."

"I may be mistaken! It is easy to misread the signs. And my lord, as I've told you it is an untrustworthy reading when your son is not yet born."

"Is this fate sealed?" Gavedon continued quietly as if he had not heard.

"No, my lord. Fate changes with every passing minute. The choices you make today will inevitably change what I have seen occurring in the future. The reading that I saw may be avoided—"

"It will be," Gavedon declared coldly, turning back around. The pleasure he had experienced when learning he was about to have a son vanished as though it had never been. "My son will not be given the tools to take my life." When the old man gasped in dread, Gavedon held up his hand. "I will not kill him, for you have warned me that this reading may be inaccurate and I would enjoy the possibility of having an heir. But he will be raised with every intent to keep the prophecy of his life from becoming true. You will tell no one of what you have seen, do you understand?"

"My lord, the Council may already know—"

"They may know that you have scryed, not what you have seen," Gavedon snapped. "Even if they threaten you with death to reveal what you have seen, you will not, old man. Just remember: I, too, have the power to take away your life. And I will find a way to do it that will not be pleasant, believe me."

"I do," the man said, shaking so hard that his grip upon the table sloshed the water from the bowl. "I will tell no one."

"Good. With any luck what you have seen will not come to pass at all, and this will be something you and I shall laugh over in years hence, yes?"

The old man laughed. It sounded pained. "Of course, my lord. Of course."

Gavedon sent him a last withering glare before throwing open the door. "Now I must deal with my wife and this 'gift' she has seen fit to give me."

The old man shivered with sympathy. Whether for the unborn son or Roisin ne Leyanon, he could not say.

Four hours later, with the wind gusting with a force that would be commented upon for days afterwards, Gavedon ni Leyanon and his wife, Roisin, were blessed with the birth of a son. Gavedon named him Hadrian.

He held the screaming child in his arms and studied the wrinkled features critically.

"If you think one day you will usurp me, you are mistaken," he said quietly. He felt Roisin's eyes upon him but he did not look at her. "You are my son and you will be obedient to me as a good son should. If you do that, I will guide you well and your name will be known across the land."

"Give him to me," Roisin said, apprehension written upon her face. Though worn from the birth, Gavedon's wife glowed with love for her son… but less for her husband.

Gavedon barely glanced at her. He did not see the beauty that had once driven him mad with want. This woman, whose hair was as pale as the snows that fell upon the Fanawel and whose ethereal face and body bespoke of flowers, was not his wife anymore. He saw a traitor.

"Rest, my love," he said, tucking the babe within his arms. "I will bring him to you after you have had proper sleep. I know you are exhausted." Ignoring her stricken moan, he carried the baby with him as he left the room.

That night in the early hours when the moon was steadily giving way to day, a single boat left the island of Shard's Point, never to return again.

The present…

"Oh, gods."

Gavedon turned to look at the woman who had moaned so forlornly. It was one of his favorites, Benta, a beautiful young woman whom Gavedon had taken to bed many times. Benta's streaming red-gold hair looked afire as the flames from Hadrian's destruction lit up the island.

Not far from where he and Benta stood, Hadrian was on his knees, crying within a blackened circle of earth. The forest was aflame. The stench of burning flesh and hair hung thick in the black smoke pressing down from above.

It was like Rhiad all over again, but Gavedon intended that he be the only one who walked away from the carnage this time.

"By the gods, Gavedon, how has it come to this?" Benta whispered, pressing her hands to her cheeks as she looked at Hadrian. "He is your son. How could he betray us like this? How could he—" she sobbed once "—how could he murder the others this way?"

Gavedon studied Hadrian, reading all the signs in that young, trembling body that told him Hadrian was near the end of his strength.

"It will be over soon," he said quietly. "I foresaw this moment and I made plans to ensure its proper conclusion. Hadrian is what I created him to be. No more. He is about to discover that to his regret."

Gavedon stepped forward and watched the familiar grey eyes swing to him tiredly.

"You've played with the others, Hadrian. Now play with me."

His son's face was filled with fear and anger in equal measure. No, this is not my son, Gavedon corrected himself. He had not thought of Hadrian as his son for a long, long time...

Nine years after Hadrian's birth...

"What do you want?"

Gavedon glared as one of the shadows disengaged from a nook in the hall. A young boy of striking beauty stepped into the light. He had the fair skin and delicate features of a girl—indeed, he looked like a young Roisin—but his inky hair and piercing grey gaze belonged to none other than Gavedon. The eyes that would forever link them together looked up at Gavedon in uncertainty.

"I would like—I would like to train with the others."

The stuttered question did not surprise Gavedon. Since Hadrian's birth he had kept his son carefully ostracized from the members of the Order. Though Hadrian was in constant passing contact with the white-robed members he was not allowed to interact with them in any way. In Gavedon's mind, giving Hadrian the education the boy wanted was akin to placing a sword in his would-be assassin's hand.

"You are bold for one so small. Has your caretaker been lapse in her duties? Are you bored, is that it?"

Hadrian shook his head. "She has been fine. I am learning much from her. But... I wish to learn what only you can teach me. I would like—" the boy blushed, "—I would like for you to teach me."

Gavedon looked him over. So the boy was lonely for his father. Satisfaction filled Gavedon. All was going according to plan.

It had been difficult raising Hadrian. Or rather, not raising him, for Gavedon had insisted that a constantly-changing retinue of members take over the raising of his son. He had decided it wisest to place Hadrian with caretakers, changing their faces so that no person remained with the boy long enough for attachments to be made. Attachments meant loyalty and Gavedon wanted his son to be loyal only to him and to yearn only for his attention. He wanted Hadrian isolated, dependent upon his father's largess for anything. It was part of Gavedon's master plan to keep his son harmless.

The other part of his plan demanded that he keep Hadrian from the mainland. Outside influences would be destructive upon a young, impressionable mind. Gavedon was not a fool; he knew that most people in Juxtan considered him a megalomaniac at best, an evil sorcerer at worst. If Hadrian ever learned of those opinions and decided that he was wasting his energy trying to win the affections of such a man, nothing would prevent Hadrian from turning on Gavedon, or at the least leaving Shard's

Point and becoming prey to unscrupulous forces that could harness his magick against the Order.

If such magick existed in the boy.

Despite the old man's prophecy, Gavedon did not sense great magick from Hadrian. Had Hadrian been another man's son and come to the island seeking instruction, Gavedon would have admitted him into the Order with great reluctance.

"I do not believe in nepotism, Hadrian." He watched the grey eyes, twins of his own, fall to the stone floor. "Unless you can prove to me that you possess the ability to magick you will not be allowed to train with the others."

"But I do have magick," Hadrian protested, raising his head. His chin lifted just slightly, an odd little show of stubbornness that Gavedon had never seen from him before. "I can feel things. Hear them."

Gavedon crossed his arms to present a formidable presence to his young son. "Such as? Be specific. Don't waste words."

Paling slightly, Hadrian said, "When I am outside of the castle, I can tell where the animals are. I hear—I hear their hearts beating." When Gavedon's eyes narrowed, Hadrian swallowed hard. "S-sometimes I think I can hear the trees too."

"Trees do not possess hearts," Gavedon said coldly.

"B-but I sense something from them. Something warm and welcoming. It—it makes me feel good."

"It makes you feel good," Gavedon repeated.

Hadrian flushed in embarrassment. "Perhaps that is not magick after all."

So Hadrian could hear Life... Gavedon was both pleased and disturbed. His son had inherited his powers. But at what cost to Gavedon later?

"I-I only wish to join the others," Hadrian went on, red-faced. "I get lonely sometimes and there are so many others in the castle that I could speak to."

"You speak to your caretaker, do you not?"

Hadrian shook his head. "I try, but she does not engage me in anything beyond my daily lessons. It is not enough. It makes me almost think she does not like me," he said miserably.

Gavedon hid his satisfaction. He had chosen Hadrian's caretakers well. He turned on his heel and continued walking down the hall, confident that Hadrian would follow as closely as a puppy begging after scraps.

"I will think on it," he said. "Prove to me you are a good son and can be an obedient student. Perhaps one day in the future there may be an opening for you to sit in on lessons."

"Oh, thank you! Thank you!"

A small hand caught his in a jubilant grip. Gavedon froze in mid-step and looked down at the pale hand holding onto his. A lump rose in his throat. Damn Roisin to the depths of the netherworld for this. She'd robbed Gavedon of the thrill of fatherhood, slashed his dreams of passing on the Order to an heir. He wanted to love Hadrian. He wanted to show pride in his son the way a proper father would.

But at what price?

Bestow love upon the one who would one day end his dream? Gavedon could not bring himself to love his murderer no matter how uncertain that prophecy might be. Though Hadrian was innocent still, Gavedon both feared and resented him. Looking upon the comely boy was to see Roisin laughing at him. Here was her ultimate jest at Gavedon's expense.

"I have changed my mind." The small hand slipped quickly from his. Gavedon could practically feel the despair and panic rolling off of his son.

"I'm sorry! I—"

"I will begin your training now. Let us go to your room."

It wasn't a far walk since they were already near the bed chambers. Gavedon was unsurprised when Hadrian jumped in front of him, preventing him from entering inside.

"Let me—let me tidy up first," Hadrian said breathlessly. His large eyes were wider still with obvious fear. "I did not have a chance to clean up after myself this morning."

Gavedon studied him. His son was a poor liar. Yet another of Roisin's traits. "Are you hiding something in there?"

Pale hands twisted against each other. "No..." Beneath Gavedon's unwavering stare, Hadrian broke. "Yes," he whispered, stepping aside.

"Thank you for not insulting me by lying," Gavedon muttered, sweeping past him and entering the small room. "I already know what it is you are hiding."

Hadrian's room held nothing of note beyond a bed, a clothes chest, and small table. It made the handmade cage which stood atop the window ledge all the more obvious.

Gavedon paused before the wooden cage and eyed the small brown bird inside. It chirped happily at him.

"I did not give you permission for this bird."

Hadrian hurried to the cage and squeezed his fingers between the bars. The bird, apparently accustomed to the boy's touch, hopped forward and nipped at his fingertips. "But look!" Hadrian said excitedly. "He is well-trained and I keep his cage clean. Please let me keep him. He keeps me company when the Order is in session. He sings!"

"You want to join the Order and you want to keep this creature," Gavedon drawled, watching Hadrian's fingers tremble before he removed them from the cage. "You ask for much, Hadrian."

"I know," his son whispered, ducking his head. "I ask more than I deserve."

"At least you are not too stupid to realize that," Gavedon said. "Very well, I will allow you to do both." He held up his hand when Hadrian's head shot up, full of delight and surprise. Gavedon imagined he almost saw love on the boy's face, though how it could have grown he had no idea. "However, you must first prove yourself worthy."

Staring at the bird and its cage, Gavedon drew upon his power, muttering words of magecraft as he did so. As he and Hadrian watched, the wooden cage sprang thorns. The thorns grew, becoming as long and sharp as claws. They continued to grow until they filled the interior of the cage and had hemmed the small bird into its center. The bird chirped and fluttered its trapped wings wildly as a thorn pricked its throat, pulling a bead of blood.

"You'll kill him!" Hadrian exclaimed, raising his hands to the cage of thorns but unable to touch it without cutting himself. "He won't sit still for that. He'll impale himself!"

"Then use the magick you boasted of earlier to free him," Gavedon replied calmly.

Desperation and a hint of betrayal darkened Hadrian's eyes as he looked back at Gavedon. "You know I cannot—"

"I know only what you claim. You say you are ready for the Order. Prove it."

He thought Hadrian would burst into tears or otherwise rail at him to release the bird. Instead, Hadrian turned back to the cage and did nothing. Gavedon waited. As the minutes stretched and the bird became more frantic in its struggle with the thorns, Gavedon began to believe that the old man had been wrong about everything. Perhaps Gavedon would get his heir, after all.

Then he felt the magick drifting into the room. Tense, Gavedon remained still as he felt the raw energy gathering about Hadrian like a storm that was gathering momentum. It was unchanneled, dangerous magick but Gavedon knew he would be able to control it if anything went awry. The question was, could Hadrian?

His answer came shortly. The wooden cage erupted into roaring flame. It looked like a ball of fire sitting upon the window sill. Hadrian screamed in horror. Gavedon's spine stiffened. He watched his dreams of an heir burn to cinder before his eyes.

Gavedon extinguished the fire with a few muttered phrases. What was left of the cage and bird looked like blackened sticks.

"No, no, no!" Hadrian whimpered, digging through the burnt wood to retrieve the black husk of his bird. "I didn't mean to..."

Gathering his composure, Gavedon moved to the door, ignoring the scene behind him. "There is one more thing you need to do before you join the training tomorrow, Hadrian." He did not turn to see if Hadrian listened. He knew that his son was. "Eat your little friend for dinner tonight. It is symbolic of the new path you are taking." He heard his son gasp. "I will see you in the morning."

He listened to Hadrian weeping as he walked down the hallway but his heart had long since closed its doors to his son. The boy back there would be the death of him unless Gavedon restrained that wild power. Gavedon would not fail to do so.

When he awoke in the morning he found a pile of bird bones picked clean, sitting outside his door. Hadrian's desire to join the Order and be closer to his father was stronger than Gavedon had expected. Kicking the bones aside grimly, Gavedon warned himself not to underestimate the boy ever again.

Hadrian was sitting in the back when Gavedon entered the prayer room. The boy looked pale and his skin carried a faint greenish cast as if eating the bird had made him sick. But he met Gavedon's eyes squarely and with a slight tilt of his chin. Hadrian was stubborn, Gavedon realized with some surprise. If Gavedon didn't mistrust him so he would have been proud.

The present…

"So let us settle this once and for all, Hadrian." Gavedon faced his son squarely. "Let us see if I have done my job well."

Hadrian's confusion was palpable. Gavedon savored it. He had given up much in trying to mold Hadrian into the heir he wanted. Now that he had so obviously failed, there was a price to be paid.

No mercy.

No guilt.

Gavedon smiled at the man across from him. "Let us begin."

CHAPTER SIX

Hadrian watched as his father moved away from Benta and the handful of members who remained. He hoped that it meant he would no longer have to fight the others. His conflict was not with them, only with Gavedon. He wanted to settle this with his father once and for all.

If only he weren't so tired.

Hadrian had used his body as a conduit for energy too many times to fight the other sorcerers. He felt hollowed out, as though someone had used a burning spoon to scrape out his insides. He had never used so much magick before. It hurt. It made his bones ache. His flesh buzzed faintly and he was afraid to touch it for fear the skin would flake and blow away. And now he had to face down Gavedon... He couldn't do it. He had nothing left.

But he had to.

Exhausted in body and spirit, Hadrian's eyes drifted away from the grim figure of his father to the men and women gathered behind him. A small frisson of surprise struck Hadrian as his eyes alighted upon a youthful face beneath a mop of dark hair. Dark brown eyes stared back at Hadrian with anger, fear, confusion—and what had been there from the beginning, four years earlier... hunger.

Time had passed, but not much had changed in some things. Hadrian's mouth fell into a tired frown as he remembered...

Hadrian's sixteenth year…

"A new member is joining the Order today."

Hadrian looked up from the pages of the book he was writing in as his father entered the lesson room with a young man in tow. The quill fell from Hadrian's nerveless fingers. The newcomer was young—only a little older than himself. Hadrian stared at the other boy with wide eyes. In all the years that he had been on Shard's Point, he had never seen anyone near his own age.

Gavedon paused before the gathered members with a hand on the young man's shoulder. The newcomer was nearly as tall as Gavedon with a shock of brown hair that fell messily over dark, brooding brown eyes framed by thick eyebrows. He had a thin face, suggesting he hadn't eaten properly in a while, and this was echoed in the loose fall of the new white Order robe over his lanky frame.

But Hadrian cared nothing for these details, fascinated by the young man's expression. It seemed to be a mixture of disdain and boredom, as if he were on Shard's Point only because he had no place better to be. It was a far cry from the usual exuberance—even gratitude—that most new members showed when first admitted into the Order. It raised Hadrian's already feverish interest in the young man. He couldn't stop staring.

"His name is Jessyd," Gavedon continued in his booming voice. "He is now one of us. As an introduction to the Order I thought we would provide Jessyd with a short lesson in drawing energy." Hadrian's heart sped up. "Everyone to the west courtyard."

Hadrian eagerly shut his book, quickly gathering his supplies.

"Not you, Hadrian."

The words robbed the energy from his movements.

Disappointed, he looked up to find Gavedon looking steadily at him.

"You will return to your study room and continue your writings."

Hadrian's eyes flicked to the new boy, and found Jessyd watching him with intensity. The apparent reflection of interest increased Hadrian's desperation.

"But, my lord, I'd like to attend the lesson with the others. Please."

"Are you refusing me?"

Hadrian flinched and saw the members nearest to him quickly move away as though he were the scene of a horrific disaster.

"N-no," he stammered as sweat trickled down his sides. He ducked his head. "I'm sorry. I'll return to my studies."

"Yes, you will," Gavedon said coldly.

Wincing at his foolhardiness, Hadrian gathered up his things and followed the others to the door. Gavedon had already moved ahead of him, guiding Jessyd to the hall that would lead to the courtyard. As the members peeled away, heading in the opposite direction, Hadrian stared after them wistfully. Gavedon had yet to allow him to sit in on a session in which the members used their magick. He had only seen Gavedon call energy twice.

Aching with curiosity and frustration, Hadrian turned and began the long trek to his study room. The study room was both Hadrian's favorite room in the castle and the room he dreaded most. At the end of a long cold hallway, he came to a stop before a large tapestry.

As he usually did, Hadrian paused to admire the depiction of his father climbing the great Fieran's Peak. Gavedon looked majestic and powerful as he held a shard of shining white rock aloft in his fist. The look on Gavedon's face, although created with simple thread, was nevertheless awe-inspiring. Gavedon looked triumphant. Proud. It was an expression that Hadrian vowed his father would one day hold for him.

He pushed aside the heavy tapestry and entered the small, circular room within. His eyes immediately shied away from the rack of whips that stood against the wall, settling instead on the worn wooden bench in the center of the room. Until Gavedon returned to begin his lesson with Hadrian, Hadrian could sit on the bench to perform his studies rather than on the floor. Compared to the stone floor, the stiff bench was a luxury.

He settled his books across his lap and opened a single volume bound in red leather. He flipped past a handful of pages covered in precise, neat writing until he found a page only half-covered with text.

This was Gavedon's history, as told to Hadrian by his father. Hadrian had been surprised and honored by his father's order that he be the one to record The One's story for later generations to read. Hadrian was continually amazed by the exploits Gavedon recounted to him. Gavedon was alternately as strong as a god and as wise as an Elder. The stories he had Hadrian write down made the younger ni Leyanon question how it was that they shared blood, for Hadrian did not feel half as accomplished nor as skilled as his father. The more he wrote of Gavedon's history in fact, the more Hadrian grew to be convinced that he was not worthy of being The One's son at all.

But writing down Gavedon's words in this room was the most intimate act father and son ever shared. Hadrian craved the moments when Gavedon's eyes lost their focus as he drifted into memory. Sometimes his father would smile in a way that was entirely unlike him. It would make Hadrian smile too, as if he shared in the secret. This was the only place Hadrian had ever heard his father laugh. In this circular room with only a small window allowing pale morning light to shaft across the floor, Hadrian saw his father the way none of the other members did and he cherished it.

But it was also in this room that Hadrian knew the most pain at his father's hand. The rack against the wall held implements of punishment that Hadrian had experienced more occasions than he cared to remember. As pleased as some of Gavedon's memories made the older man, sometimes they brought out the worst in him. If Hadrian were slow to understand a point Gavedon tried to make, if he questioned a decision that Gavedon had made in his life—or sometimes for no reason that Hadrian could discern at all—Gavedon sent him to the rack to select the instrument for his own punishment. And it didn't matter which whip he chose, because Hadrian in his desperation had tried them all. They each caused him more pain than he sometimes thought he could bear.

He set quill to ink and began writing out the last account Gavedon had given him about his fabled journey to Fieran's Peak. After an hour of careful writing, choosing words that he had found from painful practice to be the ones Gavedon preferred—describing Gavedon as 'wise' instead of 'learned', using variations of 'prophecy' whenever explaining Gavedon's choices—Hadrian straightened with a frown. He had come to the part in Gavedon's history where he and his two companions had reached Corruptor's Cross at the base of the Fanawel Mountains.

Gavedon had vaguely recounted that his two companions had fallen on ill luck and died there. But Hadrian was curious. How had they died? Why was the area called Corruptor's Cross? He didn't want to write out a simple version of events if the truth were in any way exciting. Gavedon, Hadrian had come to learn, enjoyed it when Hadrian described his actions as colorfully as possible.

Yet as he considered Gavedon's retelling of those events, Hadrian found his mind starting to drift to the newest member of the Order. Jessyd. Even the name managed to excite Hadrian. Another boy in the castle, someone who could be his friend. Hadrian had only ever taken lessons with Gavedon or with his caretaker. Perhaps his father would allow him to share lessons with Jessyd. Hadrian realized he was smiling idiotically.

The tapestry whipped against the doorway, startling him as Gavedon swept inside. The man's intimidating presence made the small room seem even tinier and Hadrian could not help it that his palms began to sweat.

"The lesson is over so quickly?" he asked, clutching his book and inkwell as he hastily stood up. Though he knew it was impossible, he feared that his daydreaming about the new boy was apparent on his face.

"Lessil is continuing in my place. There are issues concerning the new member that I need to address with you."

Hadrian felt his face heat. He looked away guiltily. "I-issues?" he stammered.

"Do not think that I missed the way you were looking at Jessyd. He is now a member of the Order just like any of the others." Hadrian cringed at the censure in his father's voice. He clutched the book he held like a shield across his chest. "You are not to consort with him without my permission. He comes from a questionable background and were it not for his considerable natural talent I would not allow him to dirty my shores with his presence."

Hadrian looked up at that statement, curiosity overriding his caution. "W-why? What is wrong with him?"

Gavedon's eyes narrowed, resembling chipped ice. He studied Hadrian far longer than the younger man was comfortable with. "If you imagine yourself befriending him, discontinue doing so, Hadrian. The Order of the White Shard is about furthering the knowledge of magick, not for arranging playmates."

Shame brought a sting to Hadrian's cheeks. "I'm sorry," he said quietly, lowering his head.

Gavedon said nothing for a long while and Hadrian feared that his father was looking over at the rack. But eventually he heard his father settle onto the wooden bench.

"Let us continue where we left off," Gavedon said calmly.

Hadrian dropped to the floor, knees knocking against the hard stones, and silently opened the book. Whatever questions he had held about Corruptor's Cross faded away as he dutifully began to write.

If there was one thing that Hadrian did well it was heed a warning. Especially one given to him by his father.

Thus when he took his place at the back of the lesson room the next morning, he was careful not to look up when he noticed from the corner of his eye that Jessyd had taken the seat next to him. It was a difficult task. He yearned to look upon a face that was young like his own. Perhaps Jessyd would even smile at him. The possibility nearly broke Hadrian's control over himself.

Until that is, he felt the unmistakable weight of Gavedon's gaze from the front of the room. Whatever urge he'd had to look at Jessyd vanished in the blink of an eye. One did not cross Gavedon lightly. Especially not Hadrian, who knew first hand the intensity of his father's wrath. He kept his attention fixed on his father and the books in front of him, studiously ignoring the curious young man seated to his left.

Today's was a difficult lesson on understanding the flow of Life's energy as it pertained to the lay of the land. Hadrian furrowed his brow as he carefully copied down as much of Gavedon's words as he could. Gavedon demanded that Hadrian be an excellent student, oftentimes testing him privately after lessons were over. Since Gavedon had not yet agreed to allow Hadrian to sit in on any of the Order's magecraft lessons, Hadrian had dedicated himself to mastering those concerning magick in the hopes that Gavedon would one day be impressed enough to agree to expand Hadrian's knowledge. Three years of learning had passed without a single lesson in magecraft, but Hadrian remained hopeful that his father would eventually change his mind.

So lost was he in copying down his father's words that Hadrian did not notice at first the small ball of parchment that skipped across his writing tablet. The next one hit his quill, smearing the letter he had been writing. Confused, he looked to the side and found Jessyd leaning forward, grinning conspiratorially at him.

Hadrian looked back at the other boy, thrilled and horrified at the same time. He glanced anxiously to the front of the room but Gavedon was busy using chalk on a writing tablet to illustrate the flow of energy at the base of mountains. Hadrian dared a glance back at Jessyd.

Jessyd scrunched up his face and rolled his eyes as he nodded his head towards Gavedon. Hadrian's mouth fell open when he realized that the other boy was making fun of his father. Making fun of The One.

Panicked, he looked back at Gavedon. The black-haired man was tracing the flow of energy as it wound around rivers.

Stop! Hadrian mouthed at Jessyd, fearful of what Gavedon's reaction would be if he caught the boy.

In answer, Jessyd made another face, this time using his fingers to pull his features into such a ridiculous expression that Hadrian had to clap his hand over his mouth to stop himself from laughing. Jessyd grinned and winked at him. Pleasant warmth spread over Hadrian's cheeks as he dared a small smile back.

Jessyd saved Hadrian from possible discovery by turning back and pretending to pay attention to the rest of the lesson. But Hadrian had succumbed to temptation. He found his eyes diverting to the boy for the rest of the day, his curiosity piqued, his loneliness momentarily abated.

Present day….

"You have no sense of loyalty, Hadrian. How disrespectful of you to turn your back on the Order this way. Have you no sense of family or friendship?"

Gavedon's words made Hadrian's head ache. Friend or family? Had he had either in this place?

"The Order raised you," Gavedon continued, shaking his head mournfully as fire continued to rage in the forest around them. "There were many you killed here who loved you."

Hadrian found himself straining forward, waiting for Gavedon to add the words he wanted to hear. But Gavedon did not profess his own love as Hadrian yearned, making the tears run hotter down his cheeks.

"All of it lies," Hadrian whispered accusingly. "You betrayed everything I believed in." As he spoke the words his eyes fell to Jessyd, the first of many disillusionments he had suffered.

The past….

Hadrian tried his best to be obedient. Gavedon would punish him terribly if he discovered that Hadrian had any contact with Jessyd. So although he drank in the sight of the other boy during their daily lessons, once schooling was over Hadrian was quick to retreat to the isolated safety of his own room. It was a difficult task, for he knew that Jessyd often tried to catch up with him. But Hadrian knew the castle as intimately as he knew the lines of his hand. In three months' time Jessyd had not been able to speak more than a passing greeting to him.

That changed though, the one day that Hadrian decided to leave the castle. It was mid-summer and the pull of the island grounds was too much for Hadrian to resist. His studies completed and assured that Gavedon was busy instructing the other members in magecraft, he ran down the stairs to the bottom floor and let himself out into the air.

It was much warmer outside than in the perpetually cool castle. Hadrian jogged into the forest and spying no one, decided to remove the heavy weight of his robe. The thin undertunic and leggings he wore beneath allowed the fresh air to cool his skin. With a sigh, he draped his robe across a patch of sun-dappled grass and followed it down.

He closed his eyes, letting the sun beat golden red against his lowered eyelids. Insects buzzed in the taller grasses above his head and he imagined he could hear the beat of the butterflies' wings as they fluttered over the flowers that surrounded him.

Life pulsed, slow and welcoming like a lazy river. He felt it beneath his shoulder blades and all along the backs of his legs. He smiled and moved his arms so that his hands fell off the robe onto the sharp blades of grass. There, he dug his fingertips into the warm, moist earth. Life's energy hummed against his fingers, traveling like languid liquid warmth into his veins. Being able to feel Life like this was the greatest gift he could imagine. He thanked the gods everyday that he was allowed to share in this sensation.

"Should I worship at your feet, I wonder?"

His eyes shot open, effectively blinding him as the bright sunlight pierced his eyes. A shadow moved to block the sun, sparing his vision.

"You look like a god of nature lying there," Jessyd remarked with a smirk. "I feel like I should be offering you some sort of sacrifice."

"What—what are you doing here?" Hadrian asked, looking wildly about him for the other members. "You're supposed to be in lessons." A horrific possibility struck him. "Oh, gods—are they here too?" Gavedon allowed him to leave the castle only with permission, which Hadrian definitely did not have right now.

"Relax," Jessyd said, stretching his long arms above his head before squatting down beside Hadrian. "I faked illness and pretended to go to my room. Gave me the chance I needed to follow you out."

"Why would you do such a thing?" Hadrian asked, genuinely mystified. Was Jessyd mad? If Gavedon found out about such deceit–

"I want to find out why I'm not allowed to play with you," Jessyd replied with a rakish grin. He had put on weight since staying at Shard's Point, the extra flesh filling out the hollows of his face and making him appear very pleasing to the eye. Hadrian blinked at his thoughts. He shouldn't be thinking such things.

"The Almighty Gavedon warned me that although I am allowed to gaze upon your miraculous beauty, I am forbidden from touching you." Jessyd snorted in derision. "How utterly preposterous. What does he think you are, I wonder? A priceless statue?"

Hadrian didn't know what to say, nervous over the fact that he was wearing his underclothing while Jessyd squatted over him fully clothed. Self-conscious, he moved his hands over his lap. Jessyd's brown eyes followed the movement and an odd heat came into his eyes.

"You truly are an incredible find on this island, Hadrian. I suppose I would do the same with you if I were in your father's place. Although he goes too far, I think. He treats you like a virginal girl, doesn't he?" Jessyd smiled slyly. "Oh, yes. He keeps you untouched in your stone castle, your virginity frozen in time. I wonder, do you wish someone would touch you, Hadrian?"

Hadrian blushed at the directness of the question and the piercing stare he received. The question seemed too intimate to answer. Hadrian knew he shouldn't be speaking with the other boy at all, much less about such things. Gavedon had forbid it.

"Please," he urged, "you should return to the castle. If Gavedon finds out how you've misled him—Or if he finds you here with me..." Hadrian looked about fretfully. "Gods, if he finds me talking to you—"

Jessyd suddenly moved forward. Startled, Hadrian fell back onto his elbows as Jessyd crawled over him. The older boy placed his knees on either side of Hadrian's hips and braced his hands beside the younger boy's head, casting Hadrian's face in shadow.

"Do you know why he doesn't want me touching you?" Jessyd murmured, looking intently at Hadrian's lips.

Hadrian shook his head, trying to use the movement to pull the other boys' gaze from his mouth. Jessyd's nearness was making his heart pound. Hadrian was afraid to breathe for fear the movement it caused would bring his body in contact with the other boy's. He clutched his hands together over his chest to ward off Jessyd as the older boy began to lower himself. "Don't!"

"He doesn't want me touching you because he knows I can make you like it," Jessyd breathed, dropping his hips. He forced a knee between Hadrian's and pried the younger boy's legs apart. "I know all the ways, you see. I used to be a whore back home." He worked his hips between Hadrian's straining legs and pressed their hips together.

The shock of Jessyd's confession was nothing compared to the shock of his body pressing down against Hadrian's groin. Hadrian jerked, his hands shooting up to push at Jessyd's chest.

"What are you doing?" To his mortification, his body swelled and hardened exactly where Jessyd's hip rubbed against him. Surely the other boy would feel it. And, gods... why was Jessyd doing this?

Jessyd grabbed Hadrian's hands and pulled them away, pinning them to the crisp grass above his head. Jessyd dropped his head, intending to kiss Hadrian but the younger boy turned his face away. Unperturbed, Jessyd settled with licking his neck.

"I'm telling you," Jessyd whispered. "I can make you like this."

Hadrian whimpered, his lashes fluttering wildly as he felt that wet slickness slide down his throat. His body was hot and sweating and he was having difficulty breathing properly. He felt sick to his stomach with nervousness and confusion. As strangely wonderful as it felt to have Jessyd atop him, holding him to the grass, the fierceness of his own reaction frightened Hadrian. He rarely touched himself, his caretakers having left him with the impression that it was something to be done sparingly and without pleasure, only for relief. To allow someone else to touch him this way surely must be ten times worse.

"My sister made me come to this tedious little island, convinced she could turn me into something more respectable than a whore." Jessyd bit into Hadrian's skin, making the younger boy give a soft moan. He smiled against Hadrian's throat. "But a whore is a whore, wherever he goes. Isn't that right, Hadrian?"

Hadrian strained against the grip on his wrists. He didn't want this. He sensed there was something wrong with Jessyd but he didn't know what. But he did know that he didn't want the older boy touching him any longer. As good as his body felt in some places, his mind was telling him that this was something dirty. And Gavedon would punish him...

"Please let me go," he gasped, pulling his face away from the persistent lips that sought his mouth. "Please, Jessyd."

The sound of his name seemed to break through the older boy's focus. He lifted his head, studying Hadrian's flushed face. Jessyd's fingers flexed once over Hadrian's wrists.

"I wouldn't be a very good whore," Jessyd began slowly, "if I had to force my partners, now would I?"

Hadrian nodded uncertainly as the brown-eyed boy grinned. The grip on his wrists disappeared as did Jessyd's weight. He blinked up into the sunlight as Jessyd walked away.

"You'll come find me when you want more. They always do," Jessyd called back cheerfully.

Trembling, Hadrian wrapped his arms about himself and watched the other boy melt into the forest. It was only after Jessyd had gone that Hadrian felt the small pain in his neck. He reached up and touched the small circle of indentations where the other boy had bitten him.

Nothing escaped Gavedon's notice for long. The keeper of the castle had eyes where he needed them and those eyes had seen what Hadrian had tried desperately to hide.

"What is that on your neck?"

Hadrian had known at once that something was wrong when he'd been summoned to the study room to meet his father. They had finished their daily lesson hours ago and retired for supper. Hadrian's meal now sat like a lump of hard clay in the pit of his stomach as he stood anxiously before his father.

"I took a nap after lessons," Hadrian began, knowing he was sealing his fate with every word, "and I must have scratched myself in my sleep."

Indeed, he had scratched himself quite deliberately in the hopes of covering up the incriminating bite mark. The result was a dark, wine-like stain that stood out like a bloody gash against his pale skin.

Gavedon eyed him in silence. Hadrian felt his face grow hotter and had to look to the stone flags as his confidence began to fail him.

But instead of calling him on the obvious lie, Gavedon said, "Indeed. I think I need a second opinion on the matter for I am unsure whether or not you speak the truth to me. You may enter," he called out loudly.

Surprised, Hadrian turned his head and immediately blanched as Jessyd shoved the tapestry aside and entered the room. The older boy's eyes widened when they fastened upon Hadrian and Hadrian knew with a sinking heart that every deceitful word he had just spoken to his father would now come back to haunt him a thousand fold.

Jessyd approached them reluctantly, eyes flicking from father to son and eventually settling upon the mark on Hadrian's throat. Hadrian could see the panic on the other boy's face and knew that Gavedon must see it too.

"I have a question for you," Gavedon said drolly, picking at a non-existent piece of thread on his robe. He glanced at Hadrian, the look so cold that Hadrian flinched. "One or both of you disobeyed my edict. I wish to know who it was." His dark head swiveled to study Jessyd, who had gone pale. "Any ideas, Jessyd? I advise you to tell the truth since your sister effectively abandoned you to my care and you now depend upon me for your... well-being."

Jessyd's mouth opened and shut. Then a curious thing happened. The fear slipped from his face, replaced with a sneer as he looked Hadrian up and down.

"Your boy found out I used to be a whore, is what happened." Jessyd waved his hand dismissively at Hadrian, ignoring the younger boy's shocked expression. "He thought he could force a free lesson from me so I had to bite him to get him off of me."

"What are you talking about?!" Hadrian sputtered, covering the bite mark with his hand. "You—you—bit me and tried to kiss me and—"

Jessyd leered at him. "Oh, come now, Hadrian. Admit it: you were so curious to know what it felt like to have sex that you couldn't control yourself. You told me yourself that you've never touched anyone before. You said you were anxious to know what it felt like." He shook his head reproachfully as Hadrian blushed an angry red. "You're lucky I'm this dedicated to becoming a sorcerer and that I listen to Gavedon's orders, else I might have let you have your way."

Hadrian shook his head angrily, stupefied by the other boy's words. Surely his father knew him better than that! But when he looked to Gavedon the elder ni Leyanon was watching him with icy grey eyes that were bereft of either warmth or understanding.

"But you can't believe him!" Hadrian protested to his father. "Surely you know I would never—"

"You lied to me about how you received that mark on your neck. Why should I believe you now?" Gavedon asked with an arched brow.

"B-but, Father—"

"Select, Hadrian."

Hadrian instinctively took a step back, his eyes darting fearfully to the rack. "Please don't," he pleaded. He glanced quickly at Jessyd and then had to look away at the amusement on the other boy's face. "Not in front of him!"

Gavedon glided to the wall near the doorway and leaned back upon it with his arms crossed over his broad chest. "Actually, Hadrian, it is Jessyd who will dole out your punishment this time. It is his person you insulted, after all."

Hadrian felt the floor drop out from beneath him. "You wouldn't," he said, aghast.

Gavedon had, in his lifetime, willfully defied every order of the Council of Elders. He could turn the sun to ice with a look. Gavedon turned that cold fury on Hadrian and Hadrian quite literally felt his knees shake. "Do not disobey me again, Hadrian."

Hadrian felt faint. Perhaps he would lose consciousness and wake up to find this was a bad dream. He staggered to the rack, the sweat cold upon his brow. With a hand that shook violently he pulled a whip with three broad leather straps from its holder. He couldn't look at Jessyd as he handed the instrument to the other boy. If he looked into the older boy's deceitful face Hadrian knew he would try to claw it.

Shame-faced, Hadrian dropped to the stones and draped himself across the wooden bench. Without prompt, he dragged the hem of his robe up until it bared his legging-covered backside. He wanted to scream, he was so humiliated. But he clutched the edge of the bench and forced himself not to make a sound. Not for Jessyd, not for Gavedon.

"Do not be afraid," Gavedon told Jessyd. "He's suffered this before when he's been disobedient. You cannot hurt him."

"Of c-course," Jessyd stammered and it was a small mollification that the other boy was nervous about proceeding.

That comfort exploded into nothingness however, at the first fall of the whip against Hadrian's buttocks. However much he was prepared for the pain it hurt badly. And differently, for the whip was being wielded by a different hand. A traitorous hand.

Hadrian hung his head, his body jolting with every lash until eventually his tears dotted the stones beneath him. Over his own choked breaths he heard Jessyd panting heavily behind him as Gavedon told him to stop and leave the room.

Once the tapestry had slapped back into place after the other boy's exit, Hadrian allowed a pained sobbed to escape his throat. He hurt, and in more than just his body.

"You did not listen to me and here you have learned why you should have." Gavedon's deep voice boomed and echoed in the circular room, shivering Hadrian's bones. "The world outside of Shard's Point is a wicked, vile place full of liars and those who would gladly hurt you. Do not trust them with anything of yourself, Hadrian. The only one you may trust that way is me."

Hadrian understood. It was his first lesson in betrayal.

"I'm sorry I disobeyed you," he whispered. "I will never do it again."

CHAPTER SEVEN

The present…

Gavedon watched Hadrian's face darken with a mixture of pain and anger as he looked past Gavedon to Jessyd. Gavedon understood the animosity. He had helped to fuel it. Jessyd had provided Gavedon with a convenient means of instilling a lesson into Hadrian. It was one that Hadrian had responded well to. Since that whipping in the study room, Hadrian had not tried to befriend another member even though Gavedon suspected that some of the others had tried, lured in by his son's appearance and the cache of being the Son of the One.

But that lesson was over with. And for now it was a distraction. This wasn't about such petty things. Gavedon stepped to the side, blocking Hadrian's view of the young man.

"Not everything was a lie, Hadrian. In fact things could have turned out differently," he said, pitching his voice so that it held a false warmth that Gavedon did not feel towards the younger ni Leyanon. "I had much hope for your future within the Order. You are my son. My heir." He heard Hadrian fail to choke back a sob. So needy, even now, Gavedon mused, fascinated. "I would never have expected this from you. I gave you everything. I shared my magick with you. Do you not remember?" Gavedon shook his head. "You scar me deeply with this betrayal, Hadrian. Deeply, indeed."

Pain flashed across Hadrian's face. Guilt.

Gavedon suppressed a grim smile. Yes, let the boy suffer. Gavedon had given him every opportunity to be the son he wanted, and at every turn, Hadrian had failed him...

Hadrian's twentieth year...

Six heavy stones levitated from the ground in front of the two white robed men who stood in the castle's courtyard. The stones flew forward to pummel the worn wall of the castle, pocking its weathered surface. A larger boulder lifted from the ground, trembling in the air as though it would fall at any moment. It steadied momentarily before hurtling forward. It hit the same wall but with less force than the stones before it had. It thudded against the wall but did not crack, falling with a heavy thump to the ground.

"Better," Gavedon said without enthusiasm. "But only just. Your performance is remarkable in its mediocrity."

Hadrian, dressed in robes that only last year had been let out to accommodate his late growth spurt, had been standing beside him in hopeful expectation. At his father's words though, the young man's shoulders visibly slumped. Frustration resumed its familiar grooves within his face. "I cannot pull more energy than that. There's nothing there for me to take."

Gavedon regarded his grown-up son with dispassionate eyes. To Gavedon's dismay, Hadrian still favored his mother, the fact becoming more obvious with every passing year. Shorter than Gavedon by several inches, with a slender build that no amount of food could fill out and soft, perfect features that were a hairsbreadth from being a female's, Hadrian was Roisin in the flesh. If it weren't for the saving graces of Hadrian's black hair and grey eyes Gavedon might have succumbed to his urges and had the young man banished from his sight forever, such was his displeasure.

But Hadrian was truly his son, if not entirely in appearance then in magickal ability. As the old seer had predicted, Hadrian could draw energy with little effort. Gavedon still denied his son lessons in magecraft, but it had not mattered. Hadrian far surpassed the abilities of the other members of the Order through sheer natural ability.

He was strong as his performance with the stones proved. But he could not pull from the heart of Life as Gavedon could. Hadrian could gather the loose, random energy that mages used, but he could not draw from Life as sorcerers did. Nor would he learn to do so if Gavedon had any say in it. Call it self-preservation. Gavedon was no fool. If he remained stronger than Hadrian he could prevent the prophecy of his son's life from coming true.

"You simply do not have the skill, it appears." Gavedon noted his son's disappointment and anger—aimed at the boy himself—that appeared often on Hadrian's face of late. Hadrian's inability to match his father's skills—along with Gavedon's unrelenting mockery of his attempts—was gradually having an effect on the young man's already shaky self-confidence. "Your progress has stalled. I'm beginning to think I'm wasting my time with you."

Hadrian flinched at the assessment but he straightened his shoulders and lifted his chin. "Let me try again. I'm sure I could do better." Though Hadrian clearly lacked in self-esteem, he hadn't yet lost his odd trait of stubbornness.

Easy to remedy. "You could hardly do worse," Gavedon said cuttingly.

Hadrian's backbone wilted. "I could try—"

Gavedon waved him off impatiently. "Yes, yes. You could try until the air screamed from your efforts but I haven't the time for such uselessness. Watch me, Hadrian." He gathered his robes about him with a long-suffering sigh, letting Hadrian know exactly how tedious he found this to be. "Watch me as I magick and tell me what is the fundamental difference between what you do and what I do." He lowered his voice as if speaking to himself, but spoke loud enough for Hadrian to understand him. "Then perhaps you will see why you are such an unrelenting disappointment to me."

Hadrian sucked in his breath, hurt. Gavedon pretended not to notice.

Heartless, cold—yes, perhaps he was both of those. But he reminded himself that he was not trying to raise a son so much as he was trying not to raise his own murderer. Hadrian required special handling which was not always conducive to familial love. Unfortunate, but true.

Not that Gavedon harbored any guilt over what he was doing. Not at all. Gavedon had always had grand visions. It was what had allowed him to take the fated steps to become what he was today. He might be hurting Hadrian now, but in the scheme of his son's life Gavedon knew he was saving Hadrian. If Hadrian didn't succumb to prophecy he would become Gavedon's heir, and that was worth any heartache the boy might suffer in the meantime. Heir to Gavedon's legacy was a priceless gift. He intended to show that to Hadrian now.

Gavedon had broken the laws of magecraft long before Hadrian was born. By that time, Gavedon had been a mage for nearly twenty years. And grown bored.

The methods of magecraft frustrated him. The basic tenets of magecraft revolved around the understanding—the absolute acceptance—that magick was meant to be a coexisting force within the natural world. Magick wasn't supposed to stir the flow of energy in the land. Magick wasn't meant to disturb at all. It was the underlying philosophy of magecraft: one should build a home into the side of a hill instead of leveling the earth to make it more accommodating.

To Gavedon, such thinking was like tiptoeing around a sleeping beast that guarded a great treasure. Yes, you weren't likely to be killed. But neither were you likely to gain access to those riches.

Energy flowed across the land like a stream, sometimes pooling as pockets of unused energy. These nodes of power were what mages tapped into, crafting spells to mold that unspent energy into something with purpose. But Gavedon considered such stricture too limiting. Why collect water from puddles when you could thrust your bucket directly into the stream?

When Gavedon had reached the top of Fieran's Peak, when he had been on the verge of his death, he had discovered the secret that had changed him forever: Life's energy didn't need to be painstakingly gathered from the ground like so many fallen leaves. It could be plucked straight from the tree. It could be taken. And by pulling from the source, Gavedon had access to unlimited power.

Sorcery! the mages cried. You steal what belongs to the gods.

"Then I am a god," Gavedon had told them. "For to turn away from such power is to be a bird content to nibble on a crumb when an entire loaf of bread is sitting there before you." From that day on he had magicked using Life's energy, and he was unrepentant.

For his audaciousness he was declared a criminal by the Council of Elders. For daring to disturb Life and take what he wanted he was considered evil. So be it. It was a small price to pay to become the One, founder of the Order of the White Shard. It was an inconsequential concern when the reward was being allowed to do this.

Life's energy rushed over him like the rays of the sun bursting over the mountains. He gasped, overcome as always by the sheer eroticism of the sensations that flooded his every nerve-ending. He could see Life glowing around him, highlighting every leaf, pulsing in every stem of a flower. His body surged to full arousal—a purely involuntary response—but one he would enjoy sating later upon one of the female members of the Order.

Hadrian didn't know this feeling. Hadrian could not tap Life this way, and was more than likely somewhat confused by Gavedon's primal responses to magicking. That was fine with Gavedon. Keeping his son a virgin in all things, even magick-induced enjoyment of the flesh, was just one more way to keep him uncertain and ignorant, dependent upon Gavedon for everything.

With his skin blazing and his heart pounding, Gavedon gazed beyond the courtyard through the one opened wall to the forest just beyond. He sent strands of magick through that opening and wrapped them around the trunk of the nearest tree. Like plucking a feather from a chicken, he tore the tree from its place in the soil. Life screamed in protest, but the wail was something Gavedon could block out from his awareness. Especially when there was something much more beautiful to listen to: that vibrant, steady beat that was the heart of Life. It was like burrowing against a mother's breast to hear that sound. It was like crawling back into the snug warmth of the womb. If threatened with its loss, Gavedon knew he would gladly trade his son's life to be able to hear it again.

Holding the uplifted tree with ropes of magickal energy, Gavedon threw it farther into the forest. As it crashed against the other trees, mowing the smaller saplings down, Gavedon cut his connection to Life's energy. He panted breathlessly, his eyes large, a grin on his face.

When he turned to Hadrian his son was staring at him in awe.

"You truly are the One," Hadrian whispered.

Gavedon nodded, his heart strumming. "And that is why you will do everything that I tell you to."

Hadrian could not pull from Life as Gavedon could, but this afternoon's lesson had left Gavedon thoughtful. He had much at stake in the Order. There were many aspirations he had left to him and many dreams that he vowed to see come true in this lifetime. Though he had learned the secret ways of extending life that only the Elders knew, such knowledge would not help him should someone decide to murder him. The seer had warned him that Hadrian would be present at his death and most likely have a hand in it. But that had been two centuries ago. In that time, Gavedon had done what he could to prevent Hadrian from becoming the type of man who could kill his own father.

But Gavedon needed to be certain.

He found the seer in his room in the east tower. The old man rarely left it now that infirmity had stiffened his joints and bent his back. Death was close at hand. It had become the seer's keeper in his self-imposed prison.

The old man's rheumy eyes looked up tiredly as Gavedon admitted himself into the bare room. Dirty plates and empty mugs littered the room's sole table. The seer did not take meals with the rest of the Order anymore. The trip down the winding stairwell had become too painful for him.

"I desire another reading," Gavedon said without preamble. "Much time has passed since the last one. I wish to know if I have successfully altered the course of my son's future."

The request was shocking enough to bring a spark of life to the old man's face. He sat up straighter in his chair and quickly put aside the book he had been reading.

"You must be mad!" the old man exclaimed, too stunned to consider the wisdom of his words. "Bad enough that we have scryed twice. To do so a third time is to cut my throat this instant. The Council cannot sit by for this again, my lord."

"You taste the dirt of the grave already, old man. What matter if the Council cuts your life short by a few months?"

The seer shook his head fearfully. "There are ways of death that are more dreadful than others. I would pass over peacefully in my bed than by the cursed magick of the Council. I will not do it. I refuse."

Gavedon weighed the gravity of the seer's will. The first time he had convinced the seer to read for him, the results had spurred Gavedon to climb Fieran's peak. Gavedon had always thought that overcoming the seer's reluctance that first time would be the most difficult. He stood corrected. He knew he would not win this latest battle by force or cajoling. A bit of incentive was called for.

Gavedon bowed his head in acknowledgement of the other man's fears. "I ask you to risk much, I admit. If my own life were not at stake, I would not be so demanding of you. But you understand my dilemma: the Order of the White Shard must continue. My teachings must not be halted by my premature death. I will not allow it." Gavedon stroked his chin, studying the older man with narrowed eyes. "You are old. Your bones ache and you cannot sleep. You have lost your enjoyment of living and I sympathize. I would like to offer you something in return for a reading. Something no man can refuse."

"I have no need of riches," the seer said quietly, warily.

Gavedon's smile deepened. "What about the riches of your youth?"

Silence settled like fog over the room. Gavedon held the seer's filmy blue gaze, watching as understanding broke slowly over the weathered old face.

"You do not have the ability," the seer breathed, sounding afraid.

Gavedon smirked. "You know I do, old man. It is as I said: the Order will continue under my lead for several centuries to come so long as nothing unnatural—" he said the word with a sneer "—happens to me in the meantime. I have the ability and I have access to the power. I can use it for your benefit."

"But only if I assist you," the seer said, bitterness tainting his face.

Gavedon crossed the room, standing over the seated man. He made his voice intimate. "You've done it twice before. Once more will hardly deepen your transgressions. You're a criminal already. But if you do it this final time you will be rewarded. You will be able to walk down those stairs again without pain. You will be able to look across the water and see the Greying Cliffs without a glass." He dropped his hand to one bony shoulder. "You will have a second chance to do all that you wished you had done in your first lifetime."

Ambivalence swung like a pendulum behind the seer's eyes. Gavedon watched the debate within and knew how close the older man was to succumbing.

He bent lower and murmured against the stringy locks of grey hair, "I know you are lonely. Perhaps you will find love this time around, old man."

The seer pulled away from him and looked up. His expression was hard. "Do not call me that. My name is Midagon."

Gavedon smiled, unapologetic. "Of course."

Present day…

"I know what you're doing," Hadrian accused. "You're trying to manipulate my feelings. I won't let you."

"Manipulate? Ah, my dear son. This is not about manipulation. It is about the fact that you have become a traitor to the Order. The term," Gavedon said with feigned sadness, "does not suit you at all."

Hadrian's face twisted. "But I would rather be that than

stand by one minute longer for this."

His eyes lost their focus, pain glazing their depths. Gavedon looked on in amusement, wondering if Hadrian was thinking of his mercenary lover who now lay dead within the smoking ruins of Rhiad.

"I should have stopped you before," Hadrian whispered, his voice cracking. "I saw it. I saw what would happen and yet I did nothing."

Gavedon snorted. "You saw the truth and you accepted it. You recognized that blood is more important than anything else in this world. Why are you forgetting that now?" He held out his hand. "Deep within you I know you are a good son, Hadrian."

Hadrian swayed toward him like a flame blown by a gust of wind. "Don't," he choked abruptly, stiffening in resolve. "Just don't! What you made me do no father should do to a son!"

Ah, Hadrian, can't you understand that there must be casualties in this war we wage?

Fittingly, Gavedon's eyes slid to the side, to the figure that stood slightly apart from the other members. He was a tall, thin man of Gavedon's age with shoulder-length sable hair lightly greyed at the temples and a handsome, if spare, face dominated by a hawk-like nose. The man was dressed in the white robes of the Order, but the expression on the man's face did not match those of his peers. Pale blue eyes looked upon the scene between father and son, unmoved by fear or anger. Gavedon could not read the expression in those eyes at all.

The past…

Gavedon set the basin upon the table, watching the water slosh gently within. "Since it will be our last, I wish a more detailed reading this time. Describe for me the exact moment of my death and who is there."

The seer, moving to stand before the basin, crossed his brows in consideration. Now that he had succumbed to Gavedon's offer the old man radiated a subdued excitement. It amused Gavedon immensely. Every man had his price.

"My readings are never more than impressions at best," Midagon replied carefully. "I see life paths, I see how they interact and I can usually tell from the change in the lifelights what has occurred. But to see something so specific as you're asking for will be difficult if not impossible. I have not the skill."

"Do you lack in skill or in power?"

Midagon raised pale blue eyes to the other man and nodded slowly, a cautious smile curling his thin lips. "Yes, I see what you mean. Perhaps if you enhance my abilities I may receive a clearer picture."

"It will be done. Begin."

The old seer, wrapped in the double warmth of his robe and a shawl, bent over the basin and allowed his gaze to lose their focus as he concentrated. There were no outward manifestations of what he was seeing for scrying was not an act of drawing magick. Midagon possessed the talent for reading signs on the magickal plane that were invisible to others. Signs that even Gavedon, who considered himself the most powerful magick user in the land, could not see.

Behind the old man, Gavedon tapped into Life, shivering as the power swept through him. His body grew taut with the force of the energy flowing into him but he tempered and controlled it with spoken words of magecraft until he had bound the energy into an invisible cape which he guided over the seer's shoulders. Gavedon then uttered a Cast of Transference which allowed the bound magick to sink into the old man's body. Midagon gasped aloud as the energy melted into him.

"I see!" he exclaimed hoarsely, clutching at the table's

edge.

"What do you see?" Gavedon demanded, sudden anxiousness getting the better of him.

"A city by the sea. Prosperous in the light of day, the bosom of death in the blanket of night."

Gavedon despised the uncertain nature of scrying. Its vagaries tried his patience. "Give me a name," he grated out.

"Many ships," Midagon murmured, blue eyes blind to this world as he watched the future enacted before him on another plane of existence. "There is a wide body of water. Not the sea... a half-moon beach that stretches to the left."

Gavedon pulled more energy, letting it seep into the magickal binding. "In which direction does the sun set?"

Midagon's eyes moved. "It falls beneath the eastern horizon. I see nothing but water when I look thus. No land to the east."

Gavedon recalled his memories of the mainland. A half-moon beach to the west... a bay... sunset in the east... a city that was farthest east...

"Rhiad," Gavedon said eventually.

Midagon instantly nodded. "Yes!"

"Why are you seeing Rhiad?" Gavedon asked.

Midagon turned his head, watching something with a seer's eyes. "A man is from this city. He is present when your lifelight ends. He has a direct hand in it, I think." Midagon's eyes widened. "His lifelight is tainted by blood and death!"

"An assassin?" Gavedon suggested impatiently. Despite his impatience he was excited. Midagon had not mentioned Hadrian, so perhaps the prophecy had changed. An assassin was simple to handle. Definitely much preferable to dealing with an errant sorcerer.

"Perhaps a soldier," Midagon corrected, his brows drawing forward. "No, he works alone. A mercenary, then. I sense many things from him."

"What does he look like?"

Midagon shuddered as Gavedon poured more magick through the link. "A handsome man... young, with hair like the sun. He catches your son's eye..."

Gavedon blinked at that, uncertain he had heard correctly. "What do you mean? Clarify."

The sharp demand had little effect on the seer who was lost into his reading. "I see their lifelights entwined. Hate and love—so much energy that it confuses me. Hadrian is there at the end... He has been with this mercenary. Their lifelights are tainted with each other... In Rhiad... you are there too, and there is death!" The seer gasped, bringing a hand to his mouth. "So much death and energy! It is massive. It is terrible—"

"What in the blazes are you talking about?" Gavedon demanded angrily as the seer's utterances became more and more random. "You're not making any sense, old man!"

Midagon shivered. "The mercenary from Rhiad follows your lifelight like a hawk after a mouse. He is relentless. And Hadrian is there..." The seer shook his head. "I don't understand."

Gavedon realized the seer was babbling. The old man apparently could not handle the full force of his readings when enhanced by Gavedon's magick.

"Listen carefully, Midagon," he said, enunciating his words carefully. "Are you telling me that it is this mercenary I should fear? That it is he who will bring my death?"

Midagon dropped his hand to the table and braced himself against it, visibly shaking with the strain of his reading. "He is the reason for everything," the seer panted, pale faced. "It is because of him that you will die."

The words were powerful. They managed to leave Gavedon slightly shaken even though he knew it was only prophecy and could be prevented. Learning that he was fated to die by the hand of a mercenary was disturbing but Gavedon quelled his fears. Twenty years ago he had been told that Hadrian would be the one to kill him. Gavedon had apparently managed to change that future. Gavedon would make certain that this too, would not come to pass.

He cut off his connection with Life and Midagon reacted as though a supporting hand had been jerked away from him. The old man collapsed against the table, knocking the basin and its contents over the edge.

Gavedon looked upon the gasping man with disgust. "I do not know if such a reading is worth the reward I offered. You left much in question, old man."

"It was the best I could do," Midagon whispered, dropping his head to the wet surface of the table. "Scrying is an uncertain art. What you have learned tonight is more than any man is allowed to."

"By edict of the Order, you mean." Gavedon scoffed at that. "Well, let the Council tear their hair out in fury, for we are about to do even more to incur their wrath." He looked the other man over, pretending to debate his next steps, though he had decided before the reading exactly what he intended. "I suppose I do owe you something for the information you have given me, however shadowy it was. I offered you your youth. You will have it." He smiled thinly. "To a degree."

As Midagon turned his head and opened his mouth to demand what Gavedon meant, Gavedon pulled from Life again, shaping it with magecraft. He used spells that were not meant to be used outside of the presence of the Council of Elders. Spells that were secret to all but a handful of trained mages. And to him.

Midagon shrieked and arched off the table as the magick hit him. Gavedon felt no pity as the other man's screams echoed off the stone walls. Magick hurt sometimes. And this was powerful magick that Gavedon used. A little discomfort was to be expected.

For long minutes, Midagon writhed in agony beneath the magick Gavedon inflicted upon him. A blue haze hovered over the twisting figure of the man as he collapsed to the floor. Skin softened and grew thicker. Hair darkened and bones solidified. Beneath the haze, Gavedon measured the progress of his magick until he deemed himself satisfied. He ended the Cast abruptly. In the ensuing silence, Midagon whimpered pathetically, his head pressed to the floor.

Gavedon looked the other man over. Midagon's hair was now a rich sable, streaked with strands of grey. Though he could not see the seer's face, the limbs that stretched the man's robes were no longer thin and bony—they held the flesh of a much younger man. A man of Gavedon's age.

You are young again, Gavedon thought at him. But that was not entirely a good thing. Midagon had come to Shard's Point while an old man, having only developed his seer's abilities in his later years. Such an ability was invaluable to Gavedon and he was pleased that he had gotten a hold of the old man while Midagon had so few years left to him and would have no more reason to travel away.

Now, though... Gavedon looked over the man's hale limbs. Midagon had the health to leave and an ability that would make him a rich man should he choose to return to the mainland. He was also a man who could reveal to others what Gavedon had been doing on Shard's Point. That could not be.

Midagon howled as a fresh wave of magick struck him. Red light enveloped the man on the floor, evidence of a terrible Cast that Gavedon had witnessed in use only once before—as a Council punishment. Something seemed to tear in the air around them, a great rending that made Gavedon flinch in brief sympathy. Midagon screamed as though his heart had been ripped from his body.

In a way, it had.

Gavedon ended the Cast, somewhat surprised to find Midagon still conscious.

"You are young," Gavedon told the sobbing man. "I

have given you what I promised."

Midagon let out a long, low wail. "But you—but you took it!" he cried out, blubbering against the stones. "Oh, gods, you took it from me!"

Gavedon felt no pity as he looked upon the other man. "Yes, I took your magick. You will never scry again, Midagon. I suggest in the years to come that you remain on the island. You are now a criminal like me, and without magick you are defenseless upon the mainland. I will offer you shelter for as long as you need it. I am not... insensitive to your predicament."

"You took my magick!" Midagon moaned, rocking upon the floor. He began to keen.

But Gavedon was already turning away from the pitiful sight. His mind was on Rhiad, and who he needed to find there.

The present…

Midagon returned Gavedon's regard blankly, not a single emotion betraying his thoughts. Since Gavedon had taken his magick from him, the former seer had become quiet and withdrawn. That was fine with Gavedon. The last thing he needed was a vengeful enemy within his own castle.

Sometimes however, such as now, Gavedon questioned Midagon's passivity. He knew Midagon held some measure of resentment towards him. He wondered how much. Well, if there was a time for Midagon to turn against him, now would be it, Gavedon decided. Hadrian was the only man who would ever confront the One so recklessly.

But Midagon did nothing and said nothing, watching the battle between father and son without so much as a twitch of the eye. The former seer did not appear to be fazed by Hadrian's tears, though in an indirect way

Midagon was responsible for them.

"You made me do those awful things and I can't let that go!" Hadrian shouted. "That cannot go unpunished, no matter if you are—who you are."

He had been about to refer to Gavedon as his father. The reversal made the elder ni Leyanon smile.

"Come, come, Hadrian. Everything that you did you did of your own free will. You said 'yes', every time. Or is your memory so short? Or so selective?"

The past…

In preparation for what he had planned, Gavedon brought Hadrian along with him on his periodic trips to the mainland for supplies. It was not so much a desire to expand Hadrian's knowledge of the world as it was Gavedon's intention to acclimatize his son to the experience so that he would not be distracted when more important business in Juxtan was at hand.

As expected, Hadrian was overwhelmed by the trips. Frightened by the Dimorada, Gavedon's fanatical worshippers who swarmed over them both upon reaching the Greying Cliffs—intimidated by the regular townspeople they came across who regarded father and son with distrust—Hadrian reacted exactly as Gavedon had hoped: he mistrusted the mainland and yearned only for a return to Shard's Point Isle.

After three such trips, Gavedon was confident that Hadrian could function on the mainland without becoming distracted by its novelties. When he felt the time was right, he sought his son in his room.

It was later in the evening than his typical visits to Hadrian, so he caught the young man unprepared. Hadrian practically fell out of his chair when Gavedon burst into the room. The book Hadrian had been reading—familiar to

Gavedon, though he could not read the spine—flew out of Hadrian's hands and skittered beneath the bed. Hadrian cast an anxious look at it before facing his father.

"It is late for you to be here," Hadrian said, clearly rattled.

Gavedon eyed him, thinking his son looked suspiciously nervous for doing something as innocent as reading, but he decided to let it pass for the time being.

"I am entrusting you with a very important task, Hadrian. Something that must be kept private between us."

Caution warred with interest on his son's face. "What is this task?"

"I wish you to travel to the city of Rhiad for me."

Hadrian's eyes grew large. "But that is so far, I've never—" His expression gave way to one of reluctance. "Is there no one else you could send in my place? You know how much I don't like traveling to the mainland. I would much rather remain here."

"But you are the only one that I trust with this," Gavedon said. "You are the only one who will do this right for me." And he smiled. "It is very important to me."

A light blush of tentative pleasure broke over Hadrian's cheeks. He had never looked more like Roisin than at that moment and Gavedon hated it. It was all Gavedon could do to keep the smile on his face as Hadrian said shyly, "Thank you for trusting me with something like this. What is it you wish me to do?"

"I need you to gather up all of the mercenaries in the city," Gavedon began. "I will give you a story to feed to them."

Gavedon explained his plan which required that Hadrian pretend to be the son of a land owner in need of a personal army. As Gavedon spoke, Hadrian's face reflected growing confusion.

"But why do this?" he asked when Gavedon had finished. "I don't understand. Why do you need them there on that day? And why am I pretending to be who I'm not?"

Gavedon stepped closer until he physically loomed over his seated son. "We are sorcerers, Hadrian. The mainland does not understand what we do. They fear it. They fear us. To admit that you have the ability to magick is to invite harm upon yourself. The disguise is for your own safety." As Hadrian paled, Gavedon continued, "As to why you are doing this, suffice to say that I have my reasons. You don't need to know them at this time. But you will. That I promise you, Hadrian. You will know everything in time."

"You promise me," Hadrian repeated, sounding somewhat stunned that his father would make him such a thing.

"And when you do this for me," Gavedon went on, all fatherly affection replaced by the steel that had made him the powerful sorcerer he was, "you will not fail me. Not one mercenary must be allowed to slip free of this net, do you understand? Not one mercenary."

Hadrian shivered as he looked up. He was afraid of his father. Gavedon gave him reason to be. Moments like this, when Hadrian's fingers trembled upon his lap and his cheeks went white, were when Gavedon felt that he had done his job well. Hadrian would never kill him. Hadrian was a lamb.

"I won't fail," Hadrian promised back. "I'll speak with every one of them."

It was a vow Gavedon knew his son would do anything to keep.

Less than a fortnight later found Hadrian sitting in the Bell and Buckle, one of Rhiad's most popular drinking establishments. He looked up at the blond stranger who approached his table and felt his heart swell with desire for the very first time.

"Heard you're looking to hire a few swords."

Back on Shard's Point Isle, a man with sable hair and light blue eyes looked out of his room at the mainland, his gaze aimed in the direction of Rhiad.

"You were a fool to keep me alive," Midagon muttered bitterly. His face was blank and his eyes were empty as he waited for the predicted tragedy to unfold.

CHAPTER EIGHT

The present…

Gavedon's words rang through Hadrian's head: You said 'yes' every time.

It was true; Hadrian had agreed to return to Rhiad. But there was a reason. A reason that had finally allowed him to understand why Gavedon took the female members of the Order to his bed. A reason that made him realize that there were other emotions in the world besides fear and disappointment and an aching need to be acknowledged.

There was lust, a treasure more precious than anything he'd been given before, and Hadrian had found it in spades in Rhiad.

The past…

The mercenary called Caledon had shown him magick. True magick. Hadrian thought it was more powerful than anything his father could show him. This magick made him fly.

It had been mere days since the golden-haired mercenary had taken Hadrian's innocence in the loft, but already Hadrian felt more connected to the older man than anyone he had ever known in the castle.

Lying in Caledon's bed, Hadrian's eyes drifted open at the traitorous thought. He shouldn't think things like that. His father was the closest person to him. Gavedon would always be. They were flesh and blood and that bond was more powerful than any link he might possibly forge with this mercenary.

But sometimes, like now as Caledon's rough fingers slid gently across his inner thigh from behind, Hadrian dared to question if his father truly cared for him. Sometimes—just sometimes—Hadrian thought he'd seen his father looking at him with something that, on any other man, Hadrian would have called malice. But that was absurd, he knew. His father was his father; Gavedon didn't hate him or even fear him—which Hadrian, on his more delusional days sometimes suspected of the man. No, Gavedon loved him because Hadrian was his son.

He had to believe that.

He had to, because otherwise he might get lost in the man who was spooned up behind him. This man who had shown Hadrian the wonders of the flesh and indeed the wonders to be found in his own body. A man whom Hadrian wanted to bring back to Shard's Point and with whom he wanted to share the same bed, the same life. Forever.

"Look at how much pleasure exists within you, love," Caledon had said to him sometime last night.

Hadrian blushed hotly to remember how Caledon had urged him to grip the footboard while the older man had slid his finger in there and touched something that had made Hadrian throw back his head and moan like a whore. In bed now, he covered his eyes with his hand, embarrassed by how he had reacted. The steady pressure of the mercenary's finger on that mysterious spot had completely undone Hadrian. He'd found release from that tiny stimulation alone.

It was a side of himself he'd never expected to find. And Caledon had been the one to bring it out.

"Why are you blushing, hmm?" Warm breath puffed over the side of his jaw, sending a tremor of excitement and anticipation through Hadrian's body. "I'm not complaining, mind you. I think you look lovely with your cheeks reddened. But it makes me curious what you're thinking to make them such."

The words made him blush even more. "I'm thinking of nothing."

Caledon chucked, sliding his hand fully along Hadrian's thigh, lifting the sorcerer's top leg and pulling it back over Caledon's hips. Hot steel that Hadrian now recognized as the mercenary's desire, poked him between the legs. Hadrian bit his lip and tried not to squirm.

"You're no liar, love, so don't even try. Were you thinking of me? I know I tend to consume a person's thoughts when I'm near."

Hadrian tried to hold it in but couldn't help but burst into laughter. "You're a bit consumed with yourself, aren't you?"

Caledon's grin pressed against his naked shoulder. "It's a conceit I've been told is justified. Don't tell me you've a mind to argue. Not after last night... And this morning."

Oh, no. Not at all. Hadrian was amazed he could remember his own name after Caledon's sensual assault, much less recall why he was here in the first place.

But he could remember, and that was the problem. He knew he had to leave soon.

He caught Caledon's hand as it wandered toward his groin. He needed to think and the mercenary had an uncanny knack for distracting him. "Did you really mean it when you said you wanted to return to my home with me?"

Caledon kissed the back of his neck. "I did, love. I don't make promises of that nature that I don't intend to keep."

Hadrian believed him. "Thank you."

Caledon's lips stilled against his skin. "For what?"

"For wanting to be with me." Hadrian was glad that he had his back to the other man. He knew his face was aflame. "I know you could have anyone you wanted."

"So could you, love, but I first to grab you and now we're both lucky. So no more of that, understand?" Warm fingers, already slicked with salve, prodded Hadrian's opening. "All you need to worry about is how full you'll be when I sink deep into you and make that pretty body mine."

"Gods..." Hadrian gasped, his ear vibrating from the deep growl placed against it.

"That's it," Caledon purred, replacing his fingers with something smooth and blunt. "Think about it, Hadrian. Think about me sliding all the way in until I can go no further. Until you can barely breathe because I'm so far, so deep inside you." When Hadrian moaned softly, overcome by the words, Caledon chuckled huskily. "You love hearing all the ways I plan to take you, don't you?"

"Just please... do it." Hadrian threw his head back as Caledon slowly entered him. Each inch felt like a mile until he felt that the mercenary had completely taken over his body. "I'll never... never get enough of this," he panted.

Caledon began to rock slowly, holding Hadrian's leg back to keep him open. "Good, because I'll never tire of feeling you so tight and hot around me. My little virgin lover." Caledon groaned, thrusting deeper. "A virgin no more."

Hadrian shuddered at the words and at the possessive pride he heard in Caledon's voice. No one had ever spoken of him this way before. No one had ever been this excited to be in his company.

When a rough hand reached around his hip and grabbed his leaking erection, he cried out and pushed urgently into the grip, teetering on the edge of release. It didn't take him long before he was tensing and then bucking into Caledon's fist as his seed spilled across the sheets.

Hadrian lay trembling on the bed as Caledon grabbed him by the hips and held him still for the mercenary's thrusts. Soon, he heard Caledon grunt harshly behind him and felt the warmth of the other man's release bathe his insides.

"We'll do this all the time," Hadrian panted, dragging Caledon's hand to his mouth and kissing it lovingly. "All the time, until you can't stand me anymore."

Caledon hugged him close. "It won't ever happen, love. You're what I want."

Hadrian smiled sleepily, listening to his lover's heartbeat against his back. "You're what I want too."

Nothing would keep them apart.

The present...

Gavedon sent a tendril of energy whipping towards him. Hadrian reflexively brought his arm up, summoning energy that felt like fire as it coursed through his nerves. He tiredly blocked the magickal attacked and stood, panting and hurting.

"You're tired, Hadrian. How long do you think you will stand up to me?" Gavedon tilted his head. "You've never felt the full effects of my power."

"No, but I've seen it at Rhiad," Hadrian spat out furiously. "When you burned those men alive."

"Self-preservation. It was kill them or risk my own death." In a softer voice, Gavedon added, "It wasn't personal, Hadrian. I wasn't deliberately trying to put an end to your love affair with your mercenary friend. I found out about him only later, remember?"

How could he forget? It was the night when everything in his life had been turned on its head.

The past…

After the painful parting with Caledon in the street, Hadrian rode out of Rhiad to a boat dock that lay midway between the city and Hanta. There, he boarded the small boat he had tied up there for the trip back to the island.

The sail gave him time to bask in the happiness he had found with Caledon. Nights found him staring up at the stars, imagining sharing the moment with the blond mercenary. Days beneath the sun he would spend touching his bare skin and pretending the touch belonged to his lover. He had grown up on Shard's Point with the sole dream of becoming a full-fledged member of the Order and taking magecraft lessons to make his father proud. That dream had changed. His thoughts of the future still included the Order, but they no longer revolved around it. The sun in his life was now a golden-haired mercenary from Rhiad.

He hoped Gavedon liked Caledon. In fact, he prayed for it. Hadrian couldn't bear to think of what would happen if his father didn't. The thought was too nerve-wracking to consider, and so he didn't.

But sharing with his father his dream of having Caledon eventually join him on the island ended up being placed on hold. Upon returning to the castle, Hadrian found Gavedon waiting for him in Hadrian's room, eager for news of the trip.

"It went well," Hadrian said, cherishing the pleasure that appeared on his father's face at the words. After Hadrian explained the success he'd had in convincing the mercenaries to be in town on the appointed day, Gavedon decided the time was right to enlighten Hadrian as to the reason for his mission.

It was not what he'd expected at all.

"You jest," Hadrian whispered.

Gavedon wasn't laughing. "I promised you a reason for your trip to Rhiad. I have given you one."

Hadrian could not wrap his mind around what his father intended to do. "But—but... no. No!" he said more forcefully. "What you want to do is terrible. It is horrible. It is... by the gods, it is nothing less than the slaughter of innocent men! You cannot be serious, Father. Please tell me this isn't true." He felt his heart creep into his voice as he said beseechingly, "Please tell me this is a joke!"

Gavedon did not appear amused in the slightest. "I told you the gist of Midagon's scrying. My fate is sealed unless this is done. Every one of those men must be killed, Hadrian. It is either they or I." Grey eyes narrowed on the younger ni Leyanon. "Or would you prefer that I be the one who dies?"

"Of course not!" Hadrian blurted anxiously. He turned away, closing his eyes. "Of course not," he repeated in a softer voice. "I would never wish you harm."

Gods, if he had known he wouldn't have agreed to go to Rhiad at all. But then he would never have met Caledon. Hadrian wanted to tear out his hair in frustration.

"Then there is no debate," Gavedon declared. "You and I will return to Rhiad and eliminate those men."

Hadrian spun, his mouth falling open. "You want me to help you in this?" He took a step back. "I can't... I can't do such a thing. Don't ask me to!" He shook his head wildly, overcome by the horror of it. "No!"

Gavedon took a step forward, making Hadrian fall back. "You are my son, Hadrian. You wish to defend my life, do you not?"

"You know I would! But this—" Hadrian shook his head, backing up. He thought of all of those men. He thought of Caledon. Oh, god, Caledon—

He jumped, startled, when his heels hit the wall of his room. He pressed back in despair as Gavedon hemmed him in. "I cannot use my magick this way, Father. Please don't make me." He shut his eyes, unable to bear the terrible demand in his father's eyes. "I cannot—kill."

Gavedon's breath was hot and fragrant with wine as it ran down Hadrian's face. "You would rather I die, is that it?"

"No! But there are—there are other things at stake," Hadrian argued lamely. The moment he said the words he knew he shouldn't have. His father was like a ferret when it came to sniffing out the few secrets of Hadrian's life. Nothing remained hidden for long. While Hadrian had planned on telling his father about Caledon eventually, now was not the time to do it.

"What else is at stake that could be more important than your father's life?" Gavedon demanded in a steely voice.

Hadrian despaired at his slip. "I met someone when I was in Rhiad," he began, daring a glance up into cold, hard eyes. He looked away again, feeling his cheeks warm as he thought about Caledon. "He became my friend, and I'd—I'd wanted to bring him back to live with us on the island. But he's... he's a mercenary."

The silence seemed to affect the air, making it too thick for Hadrian to draw into his lungs.

"Then he must die along with the others."

"No!" Hadrian shoved out from beneath his father and rushed to the center of the room. "He would never hurt you. He has no reason to. He's a kind man and light-hearted. He's no threat to you; not when he cares for me—"

Gavedon suddenly burst into laughter. "Don't tell me someone actually took an interest in you as a lover?"

Hadrian's face became hotter. "He did."

"I take it he's not very selective?"

Hadrian grew angry at the smirk on his father's face, but he didn't let it show. "He likes me well enough. And I—I like him. I don't care what you choose to say about us. He's my friend and I won't have him come to harm."

Gavedon's smirk faded. The chair at Hadrian's desk abruptly slid to the younger ni Leyanon's side, dragged there by invisible magick. A coil of rope appeared outside the window and flew in to hover above the chair.

"Sit down, Hadrian."

Magick forced him down into the chair and he didn't try to resist it. He waited with clenched jaw as the rope wound itself around his chest and his wrists, binding him securely to the chair. He glared at his father as the larger man approached and stopped directly before him.

"Someone took pity on you and showed you the ways of the flesh. Congratulations. You're a man, for what that's worth. Or perhaps a 'man' is too generous a term, considering what you and your mercenary lover did between the sheets. I doubt he was the one to lay and 'take it'," Gavedon sneered. Hadrian's hands fisted in humiliation. "Let me guess: you think that because this man was willing to paw at you, you two are in love, is that it?"

Hadrian didn't bother to answer.

Gavedon nodded knowingly. "Since you know next to nothing about these things, Hadrian, let me explain how things truly work when it comes to sex and love. When a man takes another man the way this mercenary took you he is merely sating his lusts. That's all. He no doubt found you an easy target and took advantage of you. Men do not take other men as their permanent lovers, Hadrian. It is merely a case of two animals rutting on each other for quick gratification. That is all."

"You're wrong," Hadrian bit out. "It wasn't like that at all. He was different with me."

Gavedon smiled indulgently. "Oh, Hadrian. Did he whisper sweet words in your ear? Did he tell you he wanted to spend the rest of his life with you? And after having been with you for only a few days?"

Hadrian hated Gavedon. For the first time in his life, Hadrian hated. But he didn't know if the reason he was so angry was because his father was wrong—or because he was right.

Gavedon shook his head pityingly. "He told you what you wanted to hear and like a green boy given his first taste of wine, you drank it up." His amusement disappeared and he studied Hadrian soberly. "I thought you learned this lesson with Jessyd. The outside world wishes only to use you. Whether it's your body or your magick they want, they don't really want you, Hadrian. You need to grasp that fact before it kills you. Or in this case—kills me."

Gavedon reached down and tenderly stroked Hadrian's hair. "When your mother died giving birth to you I vowed that I would keep you close to me. You are all that I have left of her in this world. I loved her so much. I see her in you and I thank the gods every day for that."

Hadrian's throat began to ache at the admission. He had never known his mother. It meant much to know that he reminded Gavedon of her.

"I wish to grow old and watch your children play on the island, Hadrian. I want you to find happiness the way I did, even if that joy with your mother was brief. But in order for that to happen you must do this thing with me in Rhiad." Gavedon let his hand dropped. "Otherwise my life is forfeit and the Order dissolves into memory."

Hadrian had never imagined having children. He had never been exposed to them and so the interest had never been nurtured. He didn't know if he wanted them. But he did know that having children meant he wouldn't be with Caledon. He wasn't willing to make that sacrifice.

"I'm sorry," Hadrian said softly. "You know how much I love you, how much I would do almost anything for you. I want you to be proud of me. I want you to be happy with me. But I—I can't do this. What you're asking of me is impossible. Surely there's some other way? I'd help you in anything else but this."

Gavedon studied him for long moments, his face unreadable. Eventually he walked to the door. "I'm going to give you a moment to think on what you're saying, Hadrian. When I return, I expect you to have changed your mind."

Midagon waited outside of Hadrian's room.

Gavedon paused as he closed the door behind him. "What do you want?"

"You are having difficulty convincing Hadrian to submit to your intentions?" the former seer ventured.

Gavedon regarded him coldly. "What does it matter to you?"

Midagon shrugged. "I came to offer my assistance. I thought perhaps the encouragement of someone other than yourself might move your son to reconsider. I thought I might also use certain magickal means to accomplish the task."

Gavedon crossed his arms. Midagon knew that Gavedon was wary of him, wondering if the former seer held any resentment towards him for stealing his magickal talent. Midagon had been very, very careful to appear otherwise.

"What is it you think to do? You no longer possess the ability to magick."

A tightening of the skin around Midagon's eyes was the only evidence that he was bothered by the reminder. He held out a fist-sized ball of glass. "Before I perfected my abilities to read in water, I used this. It is easier for me to focus on but the results are more difficult to read. I wish to use this to show your son what will happen if he doesn't help you. It won't be visually clear, but the memories of my reading for you and the emotions they created will still be very dramatic. I think the threat of what you face will be very moving for him if it becomes more than mere words."

Gavedon eyed the ball skeptically. To an untrained eye

the glass looked like nothing more threatening than a paperweight. "What do you require of me?"

Midagon held back his excitement. This was too important for him to ruin by giving the game away. "Place a Cast of Illusion on it, but altered with a Cast of Transfusion so that the images in my head will transfer into the glass. Once Hadrian sees what fate awaits you, I promise you he will submit."

Midagon counted the heartbeats as Gavedon considered the offer. When he had reached seventy-three, Gavedon nodded.

Midagon nearly crowed in triumph. He held little doubt that on his own Gavedon would eventually force Hadrian to his will. But such force would break Hadrian. It would alter him in unknown ways that wouldn't show up until much later in his future. By his expression, even Gavedon feared that.

What Gavedon didn't suspect though, was that Midagon had seen multiple futures at the tail end of his last scrying for Gavedon. Such as what would happen if Hadrian went willingly to Rhiad. Or if Hadrian did not go at all. Midagon had been careful not to share these periphery visions with Gavedon and was thankful now that he hadn't. That knowledge was the only power left to Midagon and he intended to use it to his full advantage.

"Make him see that there is no other option but to obey me," Gavedon told him gravely.

"I will show him," Midagon replied. But to himself, he thought, I will show him and find out what kind of a son Hadrian really is to you.

Hadrian tensed as the door to his room opened. He relaxed in his bindings when he saw that it was only Midagon. Seeing the old seer as a much younger man was still disconcerting to him. Such transformation was not natural. Though his father had been the one using such magick, it still left Hadrian ill at ease. Especially since Midagon did not appear to be pleased by the change. The seer stalked the halls of the castle carrying a palpable cloud of negative energy over his head.

"Midagon, have you come to untie me?" Hadrian asked hopefully, tugging at the ropes.

"I'm afraid not, my dear boy." Midagon stopped before the chair. He held a ball of glass in his hand which he held up before Hadrian's face. "Your father asked me to help change your mind."

"You know what he asks of me?" Hadrian blurted incredulously. "Do not tell me you agree with what he wants? We are not murderers here!"

"You know that I am a seer," Midagon said, the corners of his eyes pinching with some mysterious pain. "I have seen the future for the both of you. Rhiad is not something that can be avoided."

Hadrian sagged, defeated. "But he wants me to murder... someone important to me."

"It will be difficult, and I am sorry for that. This is not something done lightly and without pain. But you are a grown man and you are not wholly innocent, are you, Hadrian?" The young man's head shot up. Midagon smiled, not unkindly. "You have been stealing magecraft books from the library. You have one beneath your bed as we speak. It is thievery, but I know you did so because you wish to learn. In that same vein, one may argue that there is a valid excuse for every crime. Including that of murder."

"Murder is never excusable," Hadrian argued vehemently.

"What if it prevents further atrocities?" Midagon suggested with an arched brow. "I am here to show you that there are options in this situation, Hadrian. There are also consequences to those options." He drew Hadrian's attention to the ball. "Watch here. This is what will come to pass if you do not assist your father and you instead leave the island on your own."

Hadrian watched the glass, his eyes growing round as a nightmarish scene unfolded within the ball. "No," he protested, his heart cracking. "No, I do not want that!" He strained against the ropes binding him, his eyes filling with tears. "Please, Midagon. You can't let that happen. You can't! You don't understand!"

Midagon waited out his struggles until Hadrian slumped in his bonds. He lifted Hadrian's chin with a finger, raising the grey eyes to the glass again. "Dear boy, this is what the future holds if you do return to Rhiad and be the killer he wants you to be."

Hadrian blanched as a new scene unfolded. He thought he might be violently ill. The only thing controlling his gorge was the certainty that he would be left to sit in his own filth. The tears that had wavered in his eyes fell free to chase each other down his cheeks. His mind could barely comprehend what he was seeing. But his heart knew. His heart screamed its denial.

Midagon lowered the glass, his face expressionless. "I'm sorry for your choice," he said quietly.

Hadrian blinked up at him through blurred eyes. "I cannot make that choice. You ask the impossible. You cannot ask me to choose between such terrible fates. Midagon, you know I can't do it!"

Midagon frowned. "Gavedon did not mean for you to have a choice at all! He did not send me in here to offer you an alternative. I am supposed to make certain you do what he says." For a fraction of a moment, Midagon's face softened. "But I am giving you a choice, Hadrian. I am allowing you some free will in this, so I suggest that you use it. You may either go through with what your father wants, or I will help you to leave this island and let things fall where they may. Your decision alters your future. I'm giving you the chance to make it what you want. There is nothing worse than being a man without control over his life. Believe me in this."

Hadrian heard the bitterness in the words and he realized that his father had betrayed Midagon. He wished he could be surprised, but what he had learned of his father this day had come to change many of his perceptions of Gavedon.

"But both of those fates are worse than my own death," Hadrian replied, weary in heart and soul. "Surely you understand that. I cannot be a part of any of this. I refuse to willingly blacken my soul. I would rather—I would rather die."

The door to his room banged open and Gavedon stormed inside, his face a stone carving of rage.

Midagon fell back nervously. "My lord! I didn't realize you were listen—"

"You insolent, spineless whelp of a boy!" Gavedon snarled. His meaty palm connected with Hadrian's cheek, shocking both Midagon and Hadrian speechless. "What gave you any reason to believe that any of this revolves around you? This is about the Order of the White Shard. This is about the men and women who will be shaping the future of sorcery in Juxtan for generations to come. This is about more than your whiny, pitiful little self." He glared hotly down at Hadrian. "Take your own life? How dare you be so selfish! I have long worried that you are my son in little more than name. The cowardice and disloyalty you are showing to me now makes me believe that I was right to think such. "

Hadrian shook his head. Gavedon's words sliced away pieces of his heart. "Please don't say that..."

"Then prove me wrong," Gavedon hissed, grabbing a handful of Hadrian's hair and yanking his son's head back. All Hadrian could see was the fierce light in his father's eyes. If it was madness or passion, Hadrian couldn't tell. "Don't make me bind you to me, Hadrian. Come with me willingly and help me in this. Two sorcerers are needed for this. I need the other to be you. Prove your loyalty. Be a good son for once in your useless life. Give me one blasted reason to be proud of you."

The words ate away at Hadrian's soul. Yearning and anger warred within him—yearning for his father's approval, anger that that very need was being used to manipulate him. Against the painful pull of his hair, Hadrian managed to lower his head enough to look at Midagon, standing tense behind Gavedon.

The seer's face was troubled by the scene before him but the man's blue eyes held the stark truth. He had shown Hadrian the possibilities for the future. They burned across Hadrian's eyes, each as terrible as the other. Make a choice, Midagon had said. But Hadrian could not decide between those fates. No man could. In one, Hadrian fled the island and Gavedon burned Rhiad to the ground, killing all of its inhabitants. In the other Hadrian became a murderer, but some might have survived…

"I won't do it," he whispered, raising his gaze back to his father. "I cannot."

He had caught Gavedon by surprise for perhaps the first time ever. Again, Hadrian glimpsed that odd fear in his father's face that Hadrian thought he'd only imagined before. There was no mistaking it now. Hearing Hadrian disobey him had disturbed Gavedon.

But that unexplainable fear swiftly morphed into fury. Gavedon's fingers tightened, making Hadrian grit his teeth as his eyes teared.

"Perhaps fate is not so easy to change after all, yes, Midagon? I'm beginning to think I did not curtail your first reading after all." The mysterious comment confused Hadrian as Gavedon released him and glared down at him. Behind Gavedon, the seer did not answer, waiting warily for Gavedon's next move. "I had hoped to use this opportunity to tighten our bond," Gavedon continued. "To secure ourselves as father and son once and for all."

Hadrian felt the tears drip steadily down his face.

"But you're not the son I want. You refuse to be."

"That's not true," Hadrian argued, his voice small. But inside, he knew his father was right.

Gavedon stepped away from him. "I will give you the night to reconsider, Hadrian."

"I won't change my mind!"

Gavedon's smile broke across his lips like a splitting sausage. "Don't be so certain, my defiant son." He paused at the door and turned. "But if you insist on putting up a fight I'll add a little incentive to speed along your compliance."

Hadrian felt his head begin to tingle with the touch of magick. "What are you doing?"

When Gavedon watched him expectantly, Hadrian began breathing faster in fearful anticipation of what his father intended. Hadrian's eyes swung to Midagon. The burgeoning horror on the seer's face pushed Hadrian swiftly into panic.

It was then he felt it: a tugging at his scalp, a movement like fingers through his hair. Many fingers. Writhing fingers. Fingers that slithered and entwined across his skull.

Choking on his fear, Hadrian shot his eyes to the side as something dark dropped into the corner of his vision. A small black snake, the exact color of his hair and no thicker than his finger, danced beside his face. Another dropped down, hissing and wrapping around the first snake. Something slick slid down his temple and tried to worm itself into his ear. Hadrian cried out and thrashed wildly, tearing the skin of his wrists. He could feel his entire head moving, ropes of snakes slithering down his neck and curling around his throat. The tugging on his scalp grew stronger, pulling the skin in a hundred different directions. Hadrian heard himself whimpering.

"Ohgodsohgodsohgodsnonono!"

"Go with me to Rhiad," Gavedon said. Hadrian barely heard him, his ears filled with a sibilant whisper. "Maybe a head full of snakes will convince you that there are worse fates than saving your father's life."

Gavedon ushered a horrified Midagon out of the room and shut the door. The latch clicked just as Hadrian began screaming.

Gavedon did not leave him the night as he'd threatened. Hadrian would have claimed he'd suffered a hundred years, but the light was still purple outside the window of his room when he heard the sound of approaching footsteps.

The door to his room opened. Hadrian kept his eyes tightly clenched, unable to stand the sight of the snakes that grew from his scalp. He feared he teetered on the edge of madness. He knew he was only a few minutes away from using his magick to set his head aflame. He didn't care if it killed him.

For the last several hours he had been gritting his teeth to endure the writhing horror growing out of his head and now his jaw ached so badly he thought he'd cracked his teeth. His nails were broken from digging into the arms of his chair, and the cords of his neck stood out so thickly that pain lanced down his spine and back up into his head.

"Do you wish me to make it stop?" Gavedon asked softly.

Hadrian tried to answer coherently, but babble spilled from his lips as soon as he peeled them apart. "Please, please, stop it, make it stop, oh gods, I'll do anything, just get them off of me, get them out of me! OH, GODS, THEY'RE IN MY HEAD!"

A hand grabbed his chin. "Open your eyes, Hadrian."

He couldn't. He couldn't look at those snakes again because then it would be real and he would feel them sprouting like weeds from his skin, like worms wriggling out of his flesh, like horrible, crawling, hissing things, and oh, gods, they were in his skin—

"Open your eyes!"

Hadrian cracked open salt-crusted lashes. He found his father looking at him with pity.

"I can make them go away, Hadrian. Just agree to go with me to Rhiad and do as I say there."

Go to Rhiad, why go to Rhiad—make them stop biting me!

"Why?" he croaked.

Gavedon smiled. "To eliminate the mercenaries who threaten my life, remember?"

Oh, yes, Gavedon wanted him to help kill the mercenaries. Help kill them all with sorcery. Help kill—Caledon. And at the memory of his blond-haired lover, Hadrian recalled the futures Midagon had laid out for him. Escape with Midagon's help, or go through with Gavedon's plans. Each was a choice from hell. They were not choices at all.

But as a snake bit his earlobe, sinking tiny teeth into already abused flesh, Hadrian gradually realized that in the course of the last few hours of his torture, one choice had slowly become less awful to him.

"Go to Rhiad," Hadrian whispered in a voice raw from screaming. He blinked, expecting more tears. But he had wept himself dry.

Gavedon smiled, his thumb stroking his son's chin. "Yes, Hadrian. Will you do it willingly?"

"Kill them," Hadrian said dully.

He was tired. Too tired to think. Too tired to fight. Too tired to care what he was surrendering to. He just wanted an end to the misery, an end to the turmoil in his heart. Please stop the snakes. I'll do anything. I'll do anything—

"I'll do it," he moaned.

Tendrils of black hair, stringy with sweat, fell around his neck, their touch as soft as velvet. Hadrian sobbed with relief, his chin hitting his breast when Gavedon released him. A warm palm cupped his head and gently stroked through his hair.

"You're a good son, Hadrian. I always knew you were." Hadrian's tension-strung body slumped like a dead man's in the chair. He found himself nuzzling into his father's hand in search of comfort. "I'll have a servant draw you a bath and bring you up some food." A dry kiss was pressed to his forehead. "I want you to rest, Hadrian. We leave for Rhiad in the morning. Once we do this, you and I will have nothing to worry about ever again. Our bond will be solidified and you will never know such pain again. My poor, dear son."

The endearment echoed in Hadrian's head. He clutched it like a hand in the dark as he sank into blessed unconsciousness.

CHAPTER NINE

The present…

Hadrian reached for energy, gathering it clumsily the way an old man gathered an armful of leaves. He felt the strands slipping out of his grasp. He was frustrated by the awareness that he'd lost more energy than he'd pulled. He could do nothing about it. He was too tired to grab after them. Using what he could, he formed fire and sent it in a wave of yellow and gold towards Gavedon. For a moment the light illuminated his father's face much as it had back in Rhiad, and Hadrian shivered with dread. But unlike that fateful time, Gavedon did not fall, screaming, beneath Hadrian's attack. He deflected the fire so that it streamed in a whistling arc towards the side of the castle, crawling up the stone.

"I would have thought you'd had enough of killing," Gavedon said mildly.

Hadrian shut his eyes as dizziness swept him.

"You must have much hate inside you to want me dead, Hadrian. Patricide is a truly awful crime."

Hadrian clenched his lids tighter. "I never wanted this. I never did."

The past...

"If you are going to survive this, dear boy, you need to lock yourself away."

Hadrian had bathed and tried to eat after his father had left him. During his bath he had constantly touched his hair, reassuring himself that the strands hadn't reverted to snakes. Now, he should have been in bed, resting up for the voyage back to Rhiad in the morning. But of course he couldn't sleep. Not when he knew what he was going to do.

Midagon had entered Hadrian's room without knocking, knowing, it seemed, that Hadrian would be unable to sleep. The seer stood behind him now as Hadrian gazed out of his bedroom window in the direction of Rhiad.

"If you want to emerge from this atrocity with a shred of your honor intact, do not be Hadrian ni Leyanon when you do this," Midagon urged him.

"And who am I supposed to be if not me?" Hadrian snapped in a voice that broke. "It will be my body there. It will be my magick that delivers the blow."

Midagon stepped forward and laid a hand upon the young man's shoulder. "Be what your father wants you to be: a tool, nothing more. Do not be a man. Do not be a son. Be a tool: heartless, remorseless, without conscience. If you allow 'Hadrian' to do the things your father desires, you will be destroyed." Midagon squeezed his shoulder. "He has forced your hand as it is. Do not give him the power to ruin you. I am begging you."

Hadrian turned, bemusement on his face as he studied the seer. "Why would you beg such a thing? Why would you care what happens to me?"

"Because Gavedon ruined me," Midagon hissed. "And I have vowed with all that remains that he will not do it again while I have the wits and wherewithal to stop it." He looked deeply into Hadrian's eyes. "I have watched you grow in a manner that is unfit for a child. I have seen you stalk these halls as quiet as a shadow and as fearful as one chased by the sun. I've seen your face become a mask that shows nothing of the pain you feel when your father mistreats you, and we all know that he does," he added when Hadrian flinched. "You've a mastery of ice, Hadrian. Pull that ice around you in the days to come. Hide yourself behind the snow. Do not let your heart thaw until you are upon these shores again. Then—" Midagon's expression hardened, "—then you may unleash the fire that is within you, dear boy. Then you may extract your revenge."

"Revenge," Hadrian whispered, shocked.

Midagon nodded soberly. "It may not enter your mind now but it will. Once you have done this with him in Rhiad your heart will demand it. Be sure you have the strength to answer that call, Hadrian. Lock yourself away until then."

Lock yourself away.

Hadrian turned back to the window, the words ringing in his head. He felt the chill night air sweep over his face as if in welcome.

In the early morning hours, he gave up all attempts at sleep. He made his way silently through the castle and stood upon the shores of Shard's Point. Across the waters, golden fires danced within the guts of the Greying Cliffs. The drums of the Dimorada carried hauntingly across the surface of the sea. Hadrian could hear the men and women who lived in those cliffs singing a wild, unrecognizable song.

Did they know what he and his father intended within a few days? Were they celebrating the coming destruction? Or were they condemning it?

The night wasn't quite freezing but he felt as though he

were. Hadrian wrapped his cloak about him as the relentless wind sought every opening in his Order robes, trying to sink icy teeth into his skin. At first he begrudged the chill that his robes could not shield him from. But then he began to think more and more upon what Midagon had said to him.

The memories assailed him:

He was chopping mountains of firewood, a task his father often gave him to keep Hadrian out of his way. Hadrian raised the axe only to let it fall clumsily when he saw his father in the woods, teaching Jessyd how to magick. He watched the trees shimmer with Jessyd's magick and wanted to look away as Gavedon clapped the other boy proudly on the back. But Hadrian couldn't look away. Some masochistic part of him ordered that he watch this and remember. So he continued to watch as Gavedon turned fond eyes on a young man who was not his son. He watched and wanted to cry and scream at the injustice of it all as Gavedon loosely embraced Jessyd. Hadrian wanted to know, why not him? Why was Jessyd out there and not him?

Later...

He shivered against a draft that brought the gooseflesh to his skin as he lay curled on the stone floor outside of Gavedon's room. Hadrian listened to his father make love to Benta. He was jealous of the soft murmurs and endearments his father gave to the woman who was not his mother. Hadrian wished it were he who was being embraced. He wished it were he being spared that kind voice. He tried not to weep with longing as he heard Gavedon tell Benta that he loved her...

Once unleashed the memories poured over him, threatening to drown him in misery. All of it swelled until Hadrian realized he had no choice but to pull up the familiar ice shields or risk being swamped by the force of his anguish. If he froze his heart, he could not feel the pain. If he froze himself, he could not be reached.

By the time Gavedon sought him on the shore, Hadrian had smothered the memories so deeply inside himself that he forgot that they existed.

"All will be well, Hadrian. Once this is done the Order will continue forever, and you will be heir to my legacy."

Hadrian did not respond, his tongue encased in ice. Hadrian could not answer. 'Hadrian' was gone.

The ice cracked when they entered the town.

When he saw the familiar buildings of Rhiad sitting so innocently, Hadrian wanted to turn around and run. Never mind that Midagon had shown him that running at this point was not one of his options. He wanted to be anywhere but here.

He saw the red-haired girl at the fruit stand who had given him an apple. She was packing up her carts so she didn't see him. Hadrian urged his horse quickly past the carts, lowering his head so his hair would curtain his face.

Farther along, he saw the Bell and Buckle and a tremendous fear gripped him that the front doors would open and Caledon would step outside. Hadrian did not know what he would do if he encountered the mercenary. Hadrian would probably flee and force Gavedon to set things in motion, starting with Caledon.

He thought he might be ill.

"What a charming little town," Gavedon remarked disdainfully as he watched a woman, covered with feathers, pluck a chicken in an alley. "Perhaps we should consider burning it to the ground and eliminating the entire lot of them."

Hadrian didn't say a word. He tamped the horror of that possibility to the pit of his stomach. He pulled the ice around him. I am not here. I am not here.

Rhiad faded, blurred behind ice.

Time passed and he moved, a spectator to his own actions. Within an hour he was standing upon the dais of the Mercenary's Guild. He retreated further and further inside himself with every minute. He heard the noise in the room grow louder as mercenaries filled the large hall. Gavedon's voice buzzed in his ear as his father spoke with the greedy guild master, praising him for bringing so many men here. Hadrian coated his eyes with ice, not wanting to see faces, not wanting to see familiar golden hair...

When Gavedon at last addressed the crowd, Hadrian was far away, only a small part of him aware that Caledon must be in the room at this very instant. But by that time the ice was thick, and Hadrian could not chip through it if he'd tried.

He didn't.

The room filled with shouting. Men pounded on the doors. Gavedon leaned in close to him and said, "It is time, Hadrian."

Time. Time to face the destiny Hadrian had chosen for himself. Time to destroy his own life.

He opened his mouth and he said, "Fire."

It might have been beautiful, the way the golden flames curled and licked the air, spreading like a swarm of orange butterflies. But there was nothing beautiful in the destruction it inflicted. Or in the agony it left in its wake.

I am not here. I am not here.

It was another sorcerer who called down the fiery rain that burned the men in his path. It was another man, not he, who followed the fleeing men out of the Guild and struck them down with whipping tendrils of flame.

I am not here. I am not here.

Onto the street he and Gavedon walked, herding the mercenaries before them like hapless beasts to the slaughter. Every moving body was a target. Every building that appeared occupied was razed to the ground.

I am not here. I am not—

And then Hadrian saw him.

He pulled his eyes from the man he had just engulfed in flames and allowed them to rest for a heartbeat on Caledon.

It was the worst moment of Hadrian's life. Caledon—handsome, charming, loving Caledon—was streaked with soot and tears and was screaming out his fury. His face was a shroud of anguish and betrayal. His voice cracked beneath the weight of his pain.

I am not here. I do not see him.

But Hadrian was not alone in this massacre. And however much he wished he could turn away and pretend he had never seen Caledon, his father might be watching. So Hadrian slaughtered the part of his soul that resisted this. He sent the fire, and turned away before he had to watch it strike down his beloved.

After that, the ice was impermeable. Now that Hadrian had killed the one man who could have made a difference in his life, the remainder of the night was lost to him. He was frozen.

When he 'awoke', he found himself standing on the boat with his father, sailing back to Shard's Point Isle. Hadrian turned around to look at the mainland. What he saw made him gasp in horror. Nothing was left of Rhiad but a smudge of black smoke and yellow flickering flame. He shook his head in disbelief at the destruction he had helped to cause. It looked as if he had helped to burn the entire coast.

"By the gods, please tell me I'm dreaming," he said, aghast. "Please tell me this is a horrible nightmare!"

"You did well," was the answer Gavedon gave him. "Everything will be better from now on."

The present…

"I never wanted this," Hadrian repeated, opening his

eyes so he wouldn't have to dwell upon the images of a burning city. "I never wanted it! But I swear to you that I will face it. I will see this ended, Father. I will end this right now."

The moment he had stepped foot upon the island to the accompaniment of cheers from the other members of the Order, Hadrian lost his last tenuous grip on control. The ice had shattered. His disgust and horror over what he'd helped to do rushed over him like a wave of sewage. He'd vomited upon the shore.

He hadn't known at that moment that he would end up engaged in a magickal battle with his father, but there was no stepping back from this confrontation. Facing his father, with the castle he had been born and raised in now in flames behind him, Hadrian knew that this night could possibly see the end of the ni Leyanon line.

"If you won't allow me to turn us both in to the justice of the Council, then this must end," Hadrian declared. "I cannot allow this to happen ever again."

"You do not have the right to make such a decision," Gavedon replied with a sudden show of emotion. "You don't have the right to influence any part of my destiny! How dare you! You are nothing. You live by my grace alone!"

At that moment, Hadrian knew for certain that they would both die here.

"You will not submit to the Council?" he asked one final time, already knowing the answer, knowing that his proud, proud father would never submit to their justice.

Gavedon called energy as he said, "I would rather die."

With a hoarse shout, Hadrian pulled upon Life again. At the same time, Gavedon hurled his own gathered power. Gavedon's magickal energy reached Hadrian first, and though he managed to throw up a shield of power the force of the energy blasted Hadrian backwards through the air. He hit the ground hard and slid backwards as his chest heaved for the breath that had been knocked from his lungs.

"You do not stand a chance," Gavedon explained, pulling more energy. He began to advance on his fallen son, the air shimmering around him like an iridescent curtain. The castle and the remaining members of the Order became blurred behind the curtain of swirling energy.

"You are an untrained sorcerer." A look of satisfaction came over Gavedon's face. "And I made you that way because I knew all along that you would turn traitor to your own father. A traitor, Hadrian! The lowest of the low. And you shall be destroyed like one, your body burnt to ash so that it no longer sullies my home."

Though Hadrian understood that this had become a battle to the death, hearing his father speak such words so casually—no, so triumphantly—broke the last shred of hope he had held that somewhere inside, however deep, his father loved and needed him. Anguish bubbled up from Hadrian's throat in the form of a wracking sob. With it came the energy to surge to his feet and cry, "If there is anyone who deserves to be betrayed, it is you! You have done nothing for me. Nothing! I wish I were never born to you. I wish I didn't carry your name or your blood because both have tainted me!"

Gavedon's eyes widened with fury. With a roar he hurled energy at Hadrian. Hadrian yanked at Life, pulling useless threads of energy when he needed much, much more. The shield he threw up in defense was flimsy; Gavedon's magick smashed through it and drilled into Hadrian with the force of an ogre's fist.

The weight of the attack dashed him to the ground again, energy crackling through his nerve endings like vicious lightning, making him moan from the pain.

Drenched in fear sweat, his limbs like jelly, he nonetheless tried to climb to his feet. He could see his father advancing on him. He could feel the energy gathering in the air, making his heart beat madly. He had never seen Gavedon pulling such immense amounts of energy before. He wished he weren't seeing it now.

Hadrian managed to rise to his knees only for the next blast of magickal energy to strike him in the chest. He cried out and went sailing backwards through the air. His momentum carried him across the rocky ground, driving him into the soil where his shoulders gouged a trench in the dirt and leaves.

Once his body skidded to a halt, Hadrian lay gasping in pain. His vision blurred. He could barely draw breath. A word slipped past his lips against his will: "Father..."

But entreaty was to no avail. Energy pounced upon him like a beast. Hadrian screamed and his spine arched off the ground as fire coursed through his veins. The power came in pulses, each more painful than the last. Hadrian hadn't known Life's energy could hurt like this.

He hadn't known his father could make it hurt like this.

The pain built; layers upon layers of it. Hadrian suffered as though he were aflame. His skin sizzled. He was afraid if he raised his hand he'd see the skin curling and blackening. Yet the worst was that it burned from the inside. His blood seemed to boil in his veins. His eyes were as hot as burning coals in their sockets. He screamed and screamed as his heels and fingers dug into the ground.

Hadrian knew Gavedon could have killed him outright. The elder ni Leyanon had ended the lives of hundreds of men in Rhiad within seconds.

But he was sadistically extending Hadrian's death, and it made Hadrian furious.

Hadrian had nothing left to pull on, but he knew Life's energy was unlimited. Gavedon could pull as much as he wanted, but Hadrian had only ever drawn the same energy that mages drew upon: passive, pooled energy.

But he could draw more. He could do what Gavedon did. He had no choice if he wanted to survive this torture.

Hadrian shut his eyes against the agony of being burned alive from the inside. He concentrated and reached for the energy of Life. He found a few strings of energy but nothing that would help him. He needed more.

So he pulled.

Life resisted.

He pulled again.

There was nothing.

Hadrian's hair began to smoke. He pulled at Life again, putting his soul behind it.

On a magickal plane, he glimpsed a glimmer of energy in the heart of a sapling.

Desperate, he reached for that energy. Desperate, he did what he never would have done—he seized all of the tree's energy. And once he had it, glowing in his hand like a beating heart, he realized he could see the energy throbbing within every tree on Shard's Point. He could see the energy pulsing through the veins of the leaves. He could feel the throb of energy in the soil. The sound of Life's heartbeat was so powerful it was deafening.

Hadrian gasped and sat upright as he pulled all of that energy into him. The infusion of energy was like being reborn. Greedily, he seized everything within reach. With every hungry gulp of new energy his body sang with a pleasure that easily eclipsed the pain.

He surged to his feet, eyes wide and his body trembling with ecstasy. His heart pounded out of exhilaration and pleasure. His sex was stiff the way it had been when he was with Caledon. Hadrian was alive with that same lustful feeling. He was powerful! He could change the world with this power. He could change history.

"All this time," he whispered accusingly, his eyes finding a stunned Gavedon standing before him. "All this time, you kept this from me. All of this power was always here and you denied me this!"

Gavedon took a step backwards. "How can you—"

"Because I am a sorcerer!" Hadrian yelled at him, his voice carrying across the island like the booming shout of a giant. "I am a sorcerer, not the useless, worthless thing you convinced me I am. I will destroy you with what I can do! I will prove to you that I am something!"

Hadrian angrily formed energy—the largest coalescence of energy he had ever seen—and hurled it at his father. Gavedon immediately threw up a shield, deflecting it, so Hadrian pulled more energy and made this ball larger than the first. It hit Gavedon's shield and made it tremble. Behind the shimmer of magick Hadrian saw his father's face begin to reflect fear.

Fear was good. Fear felt good. Laughing triumphantly, Hadrian pulled from everything around him. He stripped the trees nearest him, uncaring as they shriveled and died as he stole their life energy. He pulled from the soil, and—oh, gods!—there was so much energy to be had there!

As he discovered how unlimited this power was, Hadrian couldn't stop himself from reaching for all of it. He had never felt so glorious, so powerful, so completely in control of his life. More and more energy flowed into him, drenching him like a magickal waterfall. He laughed deliriously. He threw back his head and called for more.

For once, he, Hadrian ni Leyanon, was the one with all the power. He would never be weak again. With that realization came anger. Hadrian sought Gavedon through the shimmering haze of the energy amassing to him. Hatred of a depth Hadrian didn't know he could feel rushed over him.

"Why did you treat me differently?" he demanded. "Why didn't you treat me like your son?!"

"Hadrian," Gavedon gasped, staggering backwards. "You cannot control what you are calling. Do not be a fool! Release that energy!"

Hadrian's laughed bitterly. "I'll release it. On you!"

Feeling possessed, Hadrian drew more and more power, raping the forest of its energy. When the trees could give him no more, he pulled from the earth and from the bushes and flowers. The ground shuddered beneath his feet. Hadrian pulled with growing excitement, eager to see if there was a limit to how much power he could make his own. Could he possess the power of the world? Could he become omnipotent? No one would be able to hurt him. No one could hurt the ones he loved. He could save Caledon. With this much power, surely there was a way to bring the mercenary back–

"Hadrian, you fool!"

"Shut up!" he screamed back, though now the air was nearly opaque with the tremendous amounts of energy he had gathered. He could no longer see his father or the Order. "Shut up! You deserve this. You deserve this for what you did! For killing my—my—"

He couldn't speak the words. And in truth Hadrian didn't know what to call Caledon. His lover? His love? His hope? All he knew was that Gavedon had destroyed the one goodness Hadrian had ever known.

Intense rage seethed within Hadrian, bubbling up from a source he hadn't known existed inside him. He pulled recklessly from every living source of energy on the island. He was blind to the destruction and death he left in the wake of that pillaging, wanting only to feed the demand for retribution.

The power amassed within him and soon Hadrian could no longer see, he could no longer think. He had become the magick and the pressure was so great he yearned to explode in a conflagration of revenge and despair.

Hadrian finally unleashed that power upon Gavedon, a scream tearing from his throat. And as he did so, Hadrian heard a voice within his head shriek, *Taker of Life!*

The forest detonated around him.

Hadrian screamed as his ear drums vibrated and threatened to burst. Just as quickly, the air became a vacuum, swallowing all sound. The sky went blindingly white, searing Hadrian's eyes. He cried out and threw a hand over his face. A great pressure built in the air. Hadrian was abruptly swatted to the earth by a blast of invisible power.

He lay on the trembling ground, afraid of what he had unleashed. Heat seared him. The ground shifted and groaned beneath him. The unearthly voice that had been in his head faded to a mournful wail: *Taker of Life.*

He didn't know what that meant.

If Time stopped, he did not know. Some time later, he opened his eyes again.

It was snowing.

He inhaled something down his windpipe and coughed sharply. The sound broke the eerie silence of snowfall. Bewildered at the weather, he lifted his hand and caught the dirty sleet upon his palm. But as he rubbed the thin flakes between his fingers, the snow smudged and darkened his skin.

The sky wasn't raining sleet. It was raining ash.

He climbed painfully to his feet. Now that the energy had left him, Hadrian ached from what Gavedon had done to him. His skin felt raw. His bones felt hollow. Dizziness washed over him and for a moment he thought he might faint. But he blinked back the spots before his eyes to look around him with growing confusion.

For an absurd moment, Hadrian thought he was dreaming. He didn't understand where he was. Had he been magicked to another place? He didn't recognize the blackened fields and hills that rolled out on all sides. Where were all the trees? Where were his father and the Order?

He stepped across the charred ground which was rapidly collecting a thick layer of ash that swished in the constant wind. Where was all the ash coming from? It was obvious a great fire had run rampant through here but Hadrian couldn't determine why it would still be raining down cinders when his surroundings had already burned to the ground.

Through the thick ash fall, he saw the ruins of a castle. The walls had tumbled to the ground and were smeared with soot. The huge blocks of stone rested against each other in a loose approximation of where the structure had once stood. Hadrian's step faltered as he peered into the interior of the castle. The broken furniture lying inside was that which had once been in his home.

He spun, sending up a cloud of ashes around his shins. The grey hills in the distance weren't the topography of a strange new land. Hadrian had climbed them in search of rabbits.

The dead plains which stretched to his left weren't part of a foreign desert; they had once held a path which led to the boats used for rowing to the Greying Cliffs. He couldn't see the cliffs for the ash, but he knew with rising horror that they were there.

This was Shard's Point.

A terrible question hovered on his lips but he didn't speak it. He already knew.

He had done this. He had lost control of that immense power and he had destroyed the entire island. He had burned it to the ground just like he had burned down Rhiad.

"No," he choked out, this horrific crime too much to bear on top of the other.

It wasn't possible for one man to inflict so much damage. It was impossible! Hadrian told himself he would wake up from this and find his father standing before him, mocking him for dreaming. Maybe even Rhiad had been a dream...

But the ash that brushed against his cheeks like butterflies' wings was real. The smell of smoke and burnt... things, was real. And when he scanned the ground he saw the impression of many footsteps leading to the shore and he knew that this was real too: Gavedon and the Order had survived and they had escaped. Hadrian had been abandoned on the island that he had killed.

It wasn't until one final thing clicked in his awareness that Hadrian lost all the strength in his limbs and collapsed against the remains of the castle wall.

It was the silence. The all-consuming silence. Since the day he had learned of magick, Hadrian hadn't known silence. The beat of Life's pulse had filled his being like a second heart. It had been his source of comfort in the dark, lonely days of his childhood. It had existed in his consciousness like a friend, reminding him that the world was full of wondrous entities greater than himself.

Yet now it was gone. Silenced. Because everything was dead. Or maybe... because he had lost his magick.

"Please, no," Hadrian whispered brokenly. He was at the end of his strength; at the end of his sanity. "Anything but that."

Taker of Life, he remembered hearing. Had that been his conscience speaking? Or—a sickening feeling of dread overcame him—had it been Life that he'd heard?

Hadrian fell onto his side in the ash. This was Life's punishment. He had killed the only man he had ever loved. He had attempted to murder his own father. He had stolen from Life that which was not his to take.

For those heinous crimes he had been stripped of his power and condemned to a life without magick, a life of emptiness. A life that he deserved, because he was nothing more than a criminal.

The sky continued to weep its silent tears of death but Hadrian had none of his own to share. Inside, he was as dead as his home. He closed his eyes and let himself be buried beneath the ashes. The sound of the wind was the only thing he heard.

Read more from Tricia Owens
http://www.triciaowensbooks.com

Printed in Poland
by Amazon Fulfillment
Poland Sp. z o.o., Wrocław